ALAS, PARIS

A NOVEL BY

LAWRENCE DE MARIA
(Copyright © Lawrence De Maria 2019)
Revised 2020

Dedicated to my wife, *Patricia*, without whose love,
support and faith this book
– and others –
would not have been possible,
and to my sons,
Lawrence and Christopher.
Good men, both.

Musée du Louvre is the world's largest art museum. Its 72,735 square metres (782,910 square feet) of galleries contain more than 38,000 objects. The museum started out in the 12th Century as the Louvre Castle. The magnificent edifice, with its three huge wings, Richelieu, Sully and Denon, attracts more than 10 million visitors annually, making it the world's most visited art museum. The glass pyramid, designed by I. M. Pei, is centrally located in the museum's courtyard and is where tourists enter the Louvre through underground passageways.

↓

THE KRUPP CYLINDER

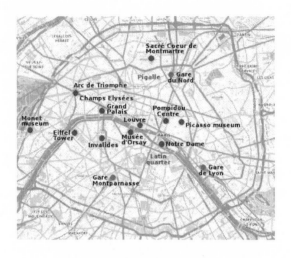

PARIS

What follows is a novel.
Did it happen?
Could it happen?
Will it happen?

PROLOGUE

On April 20, 1945, Benito Mussolini, the deposed Italian dictator, was interviewed by Gian Gaetano Cabella, an Italian journalist, in Palazzo Monforte, Milan, Italy. Mussolini was on the run from partisans and devoted much of the interview to his belief that history would revere Fascists, such as him, as martyrs. But he also spoke about his relationship with Adolf Hitler, who was then besieged in Berlin.

"I felt and feel the greatest respect for Hitler. One must distinguish between Hitler and some of his highest-ranking men. Is there still hope? Are there secret weapons? There are. It would be ludicrous and unforgivable to bluff. If the attempt on Hitler's life had not been made last summer, there would have been enough time to activate those weapons. *The famous annihilating bombs are being manufactured. I received precise information only a few days ago. Perhaps Hitler doesn't want to strike before he has absolute certainty that it will be decisive. There seem to be three bombs of incredible power. The manufacture of each one is terribly complicated and tedious.*"

***

An excerpt from an Oct. 18, 2016 *Atomic Heritage Foundation* article.

Germany had a significant head start over the

Manhattan Project, as well as some of the best scientists, a strong industrial base, sufficient materials, and the interest of its military officers.

***

Adolf Hitler

Undated

"When we are finished in Berlin, Paris will only be a shadow."

THEN

CHAPTER 1 - URANIUM MACHINE

Benito Mussolini was wrong about his legacy. He is not venerated as one of history's "martyrs". But the bombastic "Il Duce" was right about Hitler's "annihilating bombs". In fact, Mussolini had known for some time that the Germans had been working on bombs powered by nuclear fission since 1942.

Although nuclear fission was discovered by a German chemist, Otto Hahn, in 1938, many leading German physicists, particularly Werner Heisenberg, a 1932 Nobel Prize winner, believed Germany could not develop an atomic weapon in time to use during World War II. Moreover, Heisenberg's early calculations convinced him that a bomb needed at least 1,000 kilograms of purified uranium U-235 to work.

That would have made a theoretical weapon containing such a large amount of fissile uranium too bulky and too dangerous to be transported by anything less than a truck, train or ship. And that is what Heisenberg told Albert Speer, the Nazi architect and Hitler favorite, in June of 1942. With German armies stalled in Russia and ill-prepared to fight a long war of attrition, Hitler had instructed Speer to concentrate on weapons that Germany could use to win the war within a year. Speer was Minister of Armaments and War Production, and was already beginning to work the miracles of production that would keep weapons flowing to Germany's hard-pressed armies despite heavy allied bombing and the loss of conquered territories.

Even though Heisenberg told him that any German A-bomb was years away, Speer wanted to make an exception to Hitler's order. He offered Heisenberg an initial 2 million reichsmarks as seed money to develop a workable atomic bomb, with the implied promise of much more money to follow. But Heisenberg told Speer that he only wanted 350,000 reichsmarks to fund a "uranium machine" that might be useful in powering a U-boat.

Despite his brilliance, international standing, and many awards, Heisenberg was not highly regarded by the Hitler government. The Nazi press had derided him as a "white Jew" because of his friendship with purged Jewish colleagues. He even wrote letters, unsuccessfully trying to keep them out of concentration camps. Only the fact that Heisenberg's mother was a friend of Heinrich Himmler's mother, and interceded with the brutal SS chieftain, prevented his arrest and allowed Heisenberg to keep his university position.

Hitler, and most of his followers, were skeptical of what they termed "Jewish science" and the Theory of Relativity promulgated by Albert Einstein, despite empirical proof that validated his calculations. Only when the fortunes of war turned against Germany did some Nazis begin to regret having forced Einstein and other physicists to flee to the West.

Adolf Hitler, suspecting, probably correctly, that Heisenberg did not want Nazi Germany to develop an atomic weapon, decided to hedge his bets. The Nazi dictator ordered Speer to provide whatever material he could to a group of other "more-reliable" scientists working in an underground factory outside Ohrdruf, a small town near the northern slope of the Thuringian Forest in central Germany.

The factory was below a deactivated military training camp and closely guarded by the SS, which was also building a concentration camp nearby. A camp that at war's end became infamous when American generals Eisenhower and Patton publicized it after American troops discovered its horrors.

The Ohrdruf scientists reworked Heisenberg's calculations and discovered that only about 10 kilograms, the size of a soccer ball, of highly enriched U-235 could do the trick if somehow compressed into a smaller size so that its neutrons could split atoms in a chain reaction. (Heisenberg eventually reached a similar conclusion, but apparently kept it to himself.)

The problem that remained was in refining the U-235, which could start the chain reaction, out of the much-more-common U-238 found in uranium ore.

There were setbacks.

As the Nazis began overrunning Europe in 1940, a Belgian mining executive named Edgar Sengier shipped 2,000 drums of raw uranium from the Belgium Congo to a warehouse on Staten Island. The uranium ore was eventually used in the Manhattan Project to produce the atomic bombs that devastated Japan. And a commando attack in February 1943 knocked out a facility in Norway that supplied heavy-water to German scientists. Heavy-water is a form of water that contains the hydrogen isotope deuterium, and thus is 11% denser than regular water. It is not radioactive itself but can be used as a moderator in a nuclear reactor to produce plutonium from enriched uranium. Nazi scientists knew that a nuclear bomb could be fueled by plutonium as well as U-235.

Germany still had access to plenty of uranium. In fact, 16th-Century Germans are believed to have been among the first to mine Uraninite, which they called pitchblende, from silver mines in the Ore Mountains, on the German/Czech border. When Germany absorbed Czechoslovakia in March of 1939, it gained access to that nation's other uranium mines in Jáchymov, Horní Slavkov and Příbram. And when Finland became an ally after Germany invaded Russia in June of 1941, the Finns provided more uranium ore to the Nazis.

Most of the ore went to Oranienburg, a city in northeastern Germany, where Auergesellschaft, an industrial firm specializing in rare uranium and thorium, had a plant. Oranienburg, like Ohrdruf, was near notorious Nazi concentration camps, which not coincidentally supplied cheap, and expendable, labor for some of the more-dangerous uranium operations.

The Auergesellschaft plant produced tens of thousands of uranium oxide cubes, each weighing five pounds. The scientists at Ohrdruf decided on a process that used an electromagnetic isotope separator to turn the velvet-black cubes into enough fissionable uranium for three bombs.

The problem of compressing the uranium remained. The Germans used a small artillery barrel to shoot a one-gram piece of uranium into another to judge neutron emissions. The test was inconclusive (except for some Oranienburg inmates, who were killed) because the speed of the collision was insufficient to create a real chain reaction and the material blew apart, spewing deadly radiation in a massive underground chamber.

The German scientists discovered that their U-235 contained minute amounts of U-236, another uranium isotope. Unless the uranium could be further purified, the German A-bomb would not work. The Nazis were running out of time. They feared that it would be 1946 before they had enough pure U-235.

That's where Krupp AG, the huge German armaments company based in Essen, stepped in. Krupp supplied the German military with an assortment of weapons, many of which were superior to anything the Allies were able to manufacture until late in World War II. Perhaps its most-famous design was the ubiquitous 88mm artillery gun, which was adapted, with devastating effect, for anti-tank and anti-aircraft roles. The Krupp engineers fabricated a gun tube made from the welded barrels of two German 88mm guns.

The genius of the design was to have both ends of the combined barrels fire simultaneously. In an early test, the Krupp "gun" propelled two small bits of U-235 into each other at a tremendous closing speed. The resulting explosion was small, but still breached the underground chamber. The blast, and radiation release, killed more hapless concentration camp "test subjects".

It was this blast that people living in the environs reported seeing. Their descriptions of a "light brighter than the midday sun" were accurate but misled some postwar revisionist authors to claim that the Nazis had conducted a full-scale atomic test.

Surviving scientific instruments from the minor gun test measured enough fast-neutron emission to indicate that larger chunks of U-235 could go "critical". Thus, the scientists were sure the Krupp model would work as an atomic bomb. They did not see the need for a full-scale test, especially since they only had 420 kilograms of U-235 left and time was running out for Germany.

(They were not being rash or overconfident. The American "Little Boy" atomic bomb that destroyed Hiroshima on August 6, 1945 was a gun-type weapon that had never been tested. Its U-235 core was highly purified.)

The German scientists made three gun-type bombs, each with 140 kilograms of U-235, divided exactly in half. At opposite ends of the long Krupp barrel a 70-kilogram shaped charge, which the scientists called a "Teufelsstecker" (Devil's plug), would be propelled by Amatol, a conventional explosive, toward its simultaneously fired twin. The two shaped charges of U-235 would meet in the middle at a thin sheet of thorium, another radioactive metal that the Nazi scientists believed would also fission. The Ohrdurf group estimated that the explosive power of each weapon would be equal to approximately 13 million kilograms of Amatol, enough to level a medium-sized city.

(That translates into about 28 million pounds of Amatol, or 13 kilitons. The American "Little Boy" had a similar yield; 30 million pounds of TNT, or 15 kilotons.)

The Orhdruf scientists were confident that when Germany won the war with the new weapon, which they named "Rache Bombe" (Vengeance Bomb), they could refine much more U-235 and greatly improve the yield of their nuclear bombs.

One of them, a visionary theoretical physicist named Hans Draecker, even dreamed of a device using the estimated 100,000,000° Celsius temperature produced by a fission bomb to trigger the fusion of helium. Draecker's idea, for what was later named the hydrogen bomb, was not perfected by American and Russian scientists until the 1950's. Fortunately for the Allies of the 1940's, a run-of-the-mill iron bomb landed on the barracks where Draaeker was sleeping late in the war and he was blown to bits.

CHAPTER 2 - THE RACHE BOMB

The existence of Nazi Germany's atomic bombs was a secret that Adolf Hitler had first revealed to Mussolini on the afternoon of July 20, 1944 at the German dictator's Wolf's Lair field headquarters near Rastenburg, East Prussia.

Mussolini had arrived by train to be greeted at the station by a shaken Hitler, who only hours before had survived an assassination attempt made by a group of prominent anti-Nazi conspirators in a plot known to history as Operation Valkyrie. A briefcase bomb placed in a conference room had killed or seriously wounded several people, but Hitler had miraculously survived, owing to the fact that someone inadvertently moved the briefcase behind a thick wooden table support. The Führer sustained minor injuries that included a slightly injured right arm and a perforated eardrum.

In the early 1930s, before he threw his lot in with Hitler, Mussolini had been lauded as the man "who made the trains run on time" in Italy. The irony, which did not escape him, was that he was late for his meeting with the Nazi dictator. Had his train not been delayed, he would have been in the devastated conference room with his German partner!

Hitler may have been the wounded one, but Mussolini was the man who needed support. Recently rescued by German commandos from imprisonment after his ouster by the Italian monarchy, he now headed a tiny Fascist state in Northern Italy and was grasping at straws. His Repubblica Sociale Italiana was a German puppet state entirely propped up by German arms. Its capital was in Salò, a town in the Province of Brescia in the region of Lombardy on the banks of Lake Garda. The Republic of Salò, as it was derisively known, was a laughingstock among nations.

It was quite a comedown for a man once considered a mentor to Hitler in the pre-war years. Knowing that the war was surely lost, Il Duce had been urging his German ally to seek peace for months.

Amazingly, Hitler, still considered Mussolini his friend, maybe his only friend, despite the little real military support Italy had provided in the war. Perhaps he remembered how crucial Mussolini's support had been during Germany's march toward European dominance in the late 1930's, and the 80,000 Italian troops killed or captured during the German debacle at Stalingrad.

Whatever the reason, Hitler now took Mussolini into his full confidence and stiffened his spine.

The amazing revelation about Germany's atomic bomb project was made face-to-face without the presence of Colonel Eugen Dollman, the official interpreter at most Hitler-Mussolini meetings. Hitler did not speak Italian, but Mussolini spoke French and some English (he was a fan of American musicals, especially those starring Fred Astaire and Ginger Rogers) and knew enough German to get by.

Germany, working flat out since 1942 Hitler told him proudly, had managed to build three bombs, "without the help of Jew scientists", although he grudgingly admitted, he had been wrong about their theories. But owing to Allied bombing, the bomb components had been manufactured in several secret facilities across Germany. The devices now just needed their nuclear cores to be viable weapons. Hitler said he would wait for just the right moment to strike.

Unfortunately, he lamented, given its Krupp design, each "Rache Bombe" (Vengeance Bomb) would weigh more than 5,000 kilograms. Thus, it could not be flown on any surviving Luftwaffe aircraft, and certainly could not be fitted on either of Gernany's new Vergeltungswaffen (Revenge Weapons), the V-1 pulsejet or the V-2 rocket.

"That is a pity, Il Duce. Thousands of V-1s and V-2s will rain upon London, each armed with a warhead containing between 850 and 1,000 kilograms of Amatol. Enough to destroy a city block. But I do not know if they will be enough to turn the tide. The damn British are as hard to crack with terror bombing as we Germans. And we may be running out of time."

Mussolini was stunned by his friend's candor. He assumed that the shock of the briefcase bomb had something to do with that.

"But just imagine what would happen if the English capital could be destroyed by one V-2 with a warhead equivalent to more than 15 million kilograms of Amatol!"

Mussolini was flabbergasted. How was that possible? As a former schoolmaster, he knew his mathematics. Hitler was talking about a single blast equal to thousands of the blockbuster bombs the Allies were dropping on Germany and Italy.

Seeing the skepticism on Mussolini's face, Hitler

gave his friend a rare smile.

"Duce, German scientists, Otto Hahn and Fritz Strassmann, first split the uranium atom, along with Lise Meitner, a Jewess. At first, I was not convinced there could be a military application, but I funded a secret project. I don't pretend to understand it all, but apparently if you get enough of the right kind of uranium it can be made to explode by splitting its atoms. The temperatures involved are immense, millions of degrees. Needless to say, that would create an incredible blast. I was afraid such an explosion might ignite the atmosphere and destroy the planet, but my scientists say that possibility is very remote."

Remote! Mussolini certainly hoped so!

"But where did you get the uranium," he asked. "I thought saboteurs destroyed an important plant in Norway."

"Ach! That was a facility making something called heavy-water, which is used in the production of plutonium, whatever that is. Apparently that can make a bigger bomb. A setback, to be sure, but we have other methods. A bomb from uranium will do the trick. And we mined more than enough uranium in Czechoslovakia. Thank God for Munich. If that fool Chamberlain had only known, we might not have had access to those mines!"

"I still don't understand. How does one get uranium to explode with such force?"

"Ask Fermi," Hitler barked. "I understand he is showing the Americans."

That was a sore spot for Mussolini. Enrico Fermi, a Nobel Prize winning physicist and Italy's pride, had fled to the New World with his Jewish wife because of Hitler's anti-Semitic policies, which Il Duce had reluctantly enforced in Italy.

But, again, he held his tongue.

"However the infernal things works," Hitler went on, "the British will crumble and the American mercantilists will be too frightened to continue the war in Europe. They will probably turn their efforts to the Pacific, where they are apparently having their way with Japan. We will let them know they can have a free hand there, if they leave Europe. Then, Germany will turn its full attention East and bloody the Russian nose again. The war can still turn out favorably!"

Except for our dear Japanese allies, Mussolini mused.

"But how will you use the bombs? You said they are too heavy."

"By truck! I cannot reach London. And there are no worthwhile city targets in the East that I can hit now. Not that Stalin would care if he lost a city or two. In that regard, I admire the cold-blooded bastard. But I will use another bomb against the Red Army. Maybe kill Zhukov. That would stop the Bolsheviks in their tracks. Stalin has proved himself no fool. I underestimated the man."

Hitler slammed his good hand so forcefully on the side of his seat that Mussolini flinched.

"But I still control Paris," Hitler exclaimed. "I detest that bourgeois sewer, with its artistic pretensions. When it is destroyed, the Allies, especially the sentimental Americans, will turn tail. We will tell them that we have many more bombs.

What do they know? They won't risk their armies."

Paris! Even Mussolini was shocked at the thought that one of the world's most-beautiful cities would be destroyed. But his fate was so tied to the Nazi regime that he voiced no objection.

"When will these bombs be ready?"

"Soon, Il Duce. Soon. I will have to root out all the traitors who just tried to kill me. I dare not risk final assembly until all the conspirators are captured."

And brutally slaughtered, Mussolini knew.

"You spoke of a third bomb?"

Hitler gave Mussolini a wintry smile.

"I will keep it in reserve. In case my enemies need more convincing. Eventually, my scientists will build more. And they will be smaller in size, but much more powerful. They will fit atop a V-2. And then the world will again tremble before Germany!"

On his train back to Italy, Mussolini briefed the Italian officers who had accompanied him.

"It doesn't appear Hitler is planning to throw us to the wolves. The German Army is still bloodying the Allies in Italy. The Nazi General in Italy, Kesselring, is a genius."

Il Duce did not mention the Rache Bombe Hitler had bragged about. He owed his German savior that much. And he didn't trust his own generals.

CHAPTER 3 – LE CHAT À COUDRE

Created in November 1944 near the town of Ohrdruf, south of Gotha, in Thuringia, Germany, Ohrdruf was originally a labor camp. Later, it became a satellite of the notorious Buchenwald concentration camp near Weimar. Most inmates lived in stables, tents, and old bunkers, sleeping on blood-covered and lice-infected straw. Male prisoners were often worked to death in 14-hour days building roads, railways and tunnels. As the Allied armies approached, prison massacres and death marches to Buchenwald became common. About 7,000 prisoners died at the hands of the SS, the Volkssturm, and members of the Hitler-Jugend.

Obergruppenführer Ernst Heinrich nervously cocked his head toward the sound of distant thunder. But the Ohrdruf camp commander knew it wasn't thunder. He turned back to the ferret-faced man standing before him.

"How many are left Karl?"

"No more than 4,000, Obergruppenführer. We should kill them all."

Heinrich stared at Hauptsturmführer Karl Koppe. Even in the SS, Koppe was noted for his blood lust. He had been famous for the welcoming speech with which he greeted every new batch of prisoners when at Auschwitz: *"You scum are not here on holiday, but in a German concentration camp, from which the only way out is through the chimney. Jews have a right to live no longer than two weeks, Catholic priests, a month. The rest, three months. For us, all of you are not the human beings, but a pile of dung. For such enemies of the Third Reich as you, the Germans will have no respect and no mercy. You will forget about your wives, children and families. Here, all of you will die like dogs."*

At Ohrdruf, Koppe was notorious for walking around the camp and pulling out his Lugar and shooting an inmate in the head, seemingly for no reason. Heinrich had asked him about it once.

"It keeps the rest of the scum on their toes, Obergruppenführer," Koppe replied, proudly. "They will assume the dead inmate did something wrong. It is wonderful for discipline. The untermenschen, especially, then work even harder."

"Not all the inmates are subhuman, Karl."

"Of course, sir. It only seems I shoot inmates randomly. I know my targets. I only shoot Poles and Russians. And, of course, any Jews that are still around. And I try to make sure that whoever I dispatch is on their last legs, so to speak. With no more work to get out of them."

A real maniac, Heinrich realized then. So, now it was not surprising that Koppe's solution to the problem of the imminent arrival of Allied troops at Ohrdruf was simple. Murder all the surviving inmates.

"What about the women who are left?"

Heinrich had visited the barracks where the seamstresses were housed. The women there, who did important munitions work, had better rations. Some were still quite attractive, even in their shapeless concentration camp smocks.

"It's a pity they weren't killed in the factory bombing," Koppe said. "I guess we will have to shoot

21

them, as well."

Other considerations aside, Heinrich wasn't sure that was practical. Who would do all the shooting? Many of his staff, including officers, had fled. Those that stayed, fearing reprisals, were trying to make the camp somewhat presentable. A hard task, given all the corpses and bones lying about. But some progress was being made. Perhaps there was still time to avoid the hangman's noose.

"Let's hold off on that," Heinrich said. "And no more random shooting. Is that clear?"

Koppe could not hide his disappointment. The rumbling in the distance seemed to get closer. Both men looked out the window. There wasn't a cloud in the sky.

***

Like most French women her age, Natalie Filion was vain. Despite all she had been through during the war, she wondered what her liberators would think of her if and when they arrived at the Ohrdruf concentration camp. She was thin as a rail, with hip and rib bones sticking out of her 80-pound frame. Her breasts, of which she had been so proud, had shrunk to almost a boy's size by early April in 1945.

Natalie looked at her reflection in the grimy mirror above the water trough in the filthy lavatory that served the 76 women in her barracks. The mirror was a recent addition, allowed by a camp guard who, worried about reprisals from the approaching Allies, allowed the women inmates to clean themselves up a bit. In fact, conditions all over the camp had improved slightly.

Even that beast, Koppe, had not shot anyone in

days, and walked around in an obvious funk.

Natalie allowed herself a small smile. Her gaunt face did accentuate two of her finer facial traits: high cheekbones and big blue eyes. Her now slightly feline look earned her an affectionate nickname from her French compatriots: "Le chat à coudre". The sewing cat.

Natalie prayed that she had something in common with cats. After surviving Gestapo interrogations, Ravensbrück, Ohrdruf and a recent Allied bombing attack that had obliterated the camp's weapons facility where she toiled, she believed she had a few of her nine lives left.

War news was spotty inside the camp, and the women didn't know who their liberators might be. They, and the few remaining guards, hoped it was the Americans. No one wanted to be liberated by the Russians, not even the Russian prisoners.

Because of the delicate nature of their work, all the women in the weapons plant were garment workers, or seamstresses, as they preferred to be called. They came from all over conquered Europe: Russia, Poland, Hungary, France, Czechoslovakia, Greece, Yugoslavia, and Belgium. There were even some German and Italian women who had run afoul of the Nazis.

No matter what the women's country of origin was, the practical-minded Nazis wanted sure fingers handling the materials and machinery that went into the making of shells and bombs. The work was demanding, if not particularly dangerous. Amatol, the explosive used in the weapons, was inert until set off by a detonator. (Or, as was the case recently, by

Allied bombs.)

Like all the women who worked around Amatol, Natalie was allowed a shower before her shift. The water was often ice cold, and everyone had heard rumors about the soap ("I wonder who this was" some would say when they held a bar). But they all knew that no one else in the camp ever got a shower.

The women's hair had also been cut, really chopped, very short. Even then, they had to wear hair nets. The Nazis didn't want lice or other vermin to accidentally contaminate the Amatol the slave laborers molded into various shapes.

It apparently never occurred to the Nazis that accidental contamination was not the problem. The women might have appeared listless and subservient, but they still had residual patriotic energy and hated the Nazis. They certainly were not above a little sabotage.

All in all, Natalie Filion knew she and the other seamstresses were luckier than most Nazi prisoners. For one thing, they were marginally better fed than other camp inmates, which basically meant they starved more slowly.

Still, it looked as if Natalie and most of the women in her barracks might survive the war if the damn Allies got a move on!

***

On April 4, 1945, Ohrdruf was the first Nazi concentration camp liberated by the U.S. Army.

The Nazi cleanup, hampered by desertions, was incomplete. When the soldiers of the 4th Armored Division entered the camp, they discovered piles of bodies and funeral pyres stacked high with bones. No

24

senior SS officers had stuck around, and the few enlisted guards who did were summarily shot by outraged G.I.'s, or handed over to prisoners, who tore them apart while the soldiers looked the other way.

American officers radioed back to headquarters for medical help and rations. They told their men not to mix with the inmates.

But the enlisted men ignored the orders and handed out what food and cigarettes they had. Although hardened by vicious combat, many of the men had tears in their eyes. Their officers knew better than to intervene.

One American corporal from Rhode Island was approached by a young woman who grasped his face in both her hands and kissed him on both cheeks, and then on his lips.

"Amerique la belle," she said.

He remembered her blue eyes and high-cheekbones for the rest of his life.

CHAPTER 4 - ARSCH LICKER

On April 27, 1945 Mussolini, attempting to flee
from northern Italy to Switzerland in a column of
German troops, was captured, hiding in a Wehrmacht
truck, by Italian partisans. The Germans, knowing the
war was lost, happily surrendered their former ally in
return for safe passage to Austria.

The Italian strongman and his mistress, Clara
Petacchi, were briefly held in a home owned by an
Italian farming couple, Giacomo and Lia De Maria
(no relation to the author) near the small northern
Italian village of Giulino di Mezzagra.

Their respite was brief.

The next day, April 28, both Mussolini and
Petacchi were put against a wall and summarily
executed by a Communist partisan. The corpses were
transferred to Milan, where they were pummeled and
desecrated by a mob, and then hung by their heels in
a gas station.

Mussolini's famous jutting chin was
unrecognizable, as was the rest of his bloated,
disfigured face.

***

After hearing the news about Mussolini's
ignominious end on April 29, Adolf Hitler, besieged
in his dark and fetid Führerbunker, a subterranean
complex near the Reich Chancellery in Berlin,
declared: "That will never happen to me. I do not
wish to fall into the hands of an enemy who requires
a new spectacle organized by the Jews for the
amusement of their hysterical masses."

Hitler dictated his last will and testament to a

secretary, Traudl Junge. He, of course, blamed his looming downfall on the Jews.

Hitler signed the document in front of several witnesses, including Martin Ludwig Bormann, a Machiavellian sycophant known behind his back as "Herr Arsch Licker", who had become Hitler's most-trusted confidant toward the end of the war. Unlike Hermann Goering or Joseph Goebbels, he did not appear in public, and was rarely photographed. A bureaucrat through-and-through, Bormann was even in the background at Hitler's court.

The Führer instructed Junge to make three more copies of the will and bring one to his private quarters. Then, while everyone else left, Hitler told Bormann to follow him into those quarters.

Despite his anonymity, Bormann had amassed incredible power in the Third Reich. As Adolf Hitler's private secretary, he controlled all information going to and from the German leader. He relayed Hitler's increasingly raging commands, one of which was the order to arrest Heinrich Himmler (my "Faithful Heinrich!", Hitler spat) and Herman Goering, who in futile efforts to save their skins, had both tried to broker a surrender to the Allies.

That was an order Bormann relished transmitting. He hated Himmler and the obese Goering, as rivals and incompetents. He also hated Goebbels, but knew he was untouchable. Hitler adored Goebbels' wife, Magda, and was very fond of the six Goebbels children. And, Bormann reluctantly admitted, Joseph Goebbels would be loyal to his Führer to the death.

Now, Hitler and Bormann sat, a small table between them.

Hitler looked terrible. His color was ashen and his left arm was jammed in his tunic pocket, to prevent his hand from shaking. Bormann knew that the palsy was a result of both the injury the Führer had suffered during the assassination attempt the previous July and Parkinson's Disease.

Hitler began speaking about his early career and creation of the Nazi Party. Bormann had long ago become accustomed to Hitler's monologues. He knew he was not expected to speak. A smile or a nod was all the Führer wanted from his captive audiences. Bormann agonized. A million Russians were closing in and he was frightened.

He wanted to leave the bunker if he could. During his rise in power, Bormann had assumed the title of Head of the Parteikanzlei and had virtual control over all domestic matters. He had also promoted brutal treatment of Jews and Slavs in the areas conquered by Germany, areas now liberated by a vengeful Red Army.

If captured, Bormann assumed his anonymity would vanish. He thus had few illusions about his fate.

A half hour passed. Hitler was now describing what was his greatest triumph. The defeat of France in 1940. He spoke of his visit to Paris then, the only time he had been in the city. Suddenly, Hitler blurted out:

"Bormann, you are the last man I can trust. I may die in Berlin."

That deserved more than a nod.

"No, my Führer! There is still hope. After all, Roosevelt is dead."

The news of the American President's death from a cerebral hemorrhage on April 12 had briefly energized the people in the bunker with the hope that the Western alliance with the Soviets would collapse. But only their hope collapsed.

It was as if Hitler did not hear him.

"If things turn out badly, Bormann, I want you to escape. I will have an important assignment for you."

The order was music to the ears of the frightened satrap.

"But I want to stay by your side, my Führer," Bormann said with as much false sincerity as he could muster.

"I doubt that, Bormann."

Hitler even managed a small smile.

"You are a born survivor, which is why I have chosen you. Everyone else has betrayed me. Choltitz disobeyed my direct order. He let the Americans and their puppet, De Gaulle, into Paris, instead of destroying it. But I will have the last laugh on all of them."

Bormann knew who Generalleutnant Dietrich von Choltitz was. The portly general, the antithesis of Aryan manhood, had nevertheless won Hitler's admiration for his service in Normandy and given command of Paris. Yet, von Choltitz had defied his Führer's order to destroy the city. And Bormann also knew that Hitler hated De Gaulle and the French, who were about to reap rewards won by others on the battlefield.

But that was all ancient history. Bormann was about to ask just what he was "chosen" for when they were interrupted by a single knock on the door, quickly followed by three quick raps. Obviously, a signal.

Hitler got up and opened the door himself. Bormann caught a glance of Traudl Junge, who handed the Führer a small sheaf of papers.

"Danke, Traudl," Hitler said politely.

It always amazed Bormann how much deference the Nazi leader, who had consigned so many millions to death, showed to women in his circle.

Hitler turned to him.

"There is a Hauptmann Amann somewhere in the bunker. Send him to me at once!"

Bormann jumped to his feet, snapped off a "Heil Hitler" salute and quickly left.

CHAPTER 5 - EVA'S BIBLE

Bormann again entered Hitler's quarters. This time, he was not asked to sit. A large wooden Victrola in the corner of the room was blaring Richard Wagner's *Götterdämmerung*, from the composer's masterpiece, *The Ring of the Nibelungen*.

"The time has come, Bormann," Hitler said, pointing at the Victrola, which technicians had somehow managed to keep in excellent condition, judging by its clear sound. "It is indeed *The Twilight of the Gods*".

Bormann couldn't help noticing that the drums on the record were nicely augmented by occasional burst of a Russian artillery shell in the courtyard above.

There was a large yellow envelope on the table. It was embossed with Hitler's personal emblem, a Swastika with "A" on one side and "H" on the other. Bormann could see that it contained some material.

The Nazi leader picked up the envelope with his right hand. His left arm came out of his tunic pocket and he produced a small piece of paper, which he shakily handed to Bormann.

"It is from Eva's bible," Hitler explained, with a rueful smile. "She still clings to childhood fantasies."

The surprise must have shown on his face. Everyone knew that the Führer, despite being raised a Catholic, despised religion, as did Bormann. In fact, he was the chief supporter of Hitler's persecution of Christian churches.

Eva Braun was one of the few people in the Führer's inner circle that Bormann truly liked. She had always treated him decently. He knew her to be a woman of simple tastes who did not threaten Hitler's immense ego, or, more importantly, Bormann's influence. Hitler had married her earlier that day, with Bormann in attendance.

"I let her keep it. The book gives her comfort, though she rarely reads it, if at all. She never even missed the page I removed. Just as well. She would be angry over my 'desecration' of this claptrap."

There was another rumbling of Russian shells exploding overhead. Hitler nodded to the ceiling and looked rueful.

"I have enough people mad at me."

Married only a few hours, and already henpecked, Bormann thought. He turned his attention to the bible fragment. He read:

"And after these things I saw another angel come down from heaven, having great power; and the earth was lightened with his glory.

And he cried mightily with a strong voice, saying, Babylon the great is fallen, is fallen, and is become the habitation of devils, and the hold of every foul spirit, and a cage of every unclean and hateful bird.

For all nations have drunk of the wine of the wrath of her fornication, and the kings of the earth have committed fornication with her, and the merchants of the earth are waxed rich through the abundance of her delicacies.

And I heard another voice from heaven, saying, Come out of her, my people, that ye be not partakers of her sins, and that ye receive not of her plagues.

For her sins have reached unto heaven, and God hath remembered her iniquities.

Reward her even as she rewarded you, and double unto her double according to her works: in the cup which she hath filled fill to her double.

How much she hath glorified herself, and lived deliciously, so much torment and sorrow give her: for she saith in her heart, I sit a queen, and am no widow, and shall see no sorrow.

Therefore shall her plagues come in one day, death, and mourning, and famine; and she shall be utterly burned with fire: for strong is the Lord God who judgeth her.

And the kings of the earth, who have committed fornication and lived deliciously with her, shall bewail her, and lament for her, when they shall see the smoke of her burning,

Standing afar off for the fear of her torment, saying, Alas, alas, that great city Babylon, that mighty city! for in one hour is thy judgment come.

And the merchants of the earth shall weep and mourn over her; for no man buyeth their merchandise any more:

The merchandise of gold, and silver, and precious stones, and of pearls, and fine linen, and purple, and silk, and scarlet, and all thyine wood, and all manner vessels of ivory, and all manner vessels of most precious wood, and of brass, and iron, and marble,"

The script ended there. It was obvious that some of the page had been neatly cut off.

"The Old Testament," Hitler explained. "The Book of Revelations. The Jews talk about the destruction of Babylon."

Hitler became agitated.

"*Thy judgment come*, indeed! They were off by about two millenniums!"

He calmed down.

"Anyway, this is the top half of the page. You must make sure that it is reunited with the bottom half!"

"Where is the rest of it, my Führer?"

Hitler ignored the question. He took the bible fragment from Bormann and shakily placed it in the envelope and then sealed it. He then handed the envelope to Bormann.

"Now, listen carefully. I have made arrangements."

Bormann listened, as if his life depended on it. Which, of course, it did. When Hitler finished, Bormann asked the obvious question.

"But, how will I get to Stendahl?"

"Hauptmann Amann and his men will get you through to Nauen. It is not far. You will be met there. When you get to Stendahl, you will be safe."

Bormann was encouraged. Hitler did not use the word Hauptsturmführer, the term for an SS captain. Amann sounded like regular Wehrmacht. That meant he was probably levelheaded, unlike SS officers who preferred death in battle.

"What of my family, my Führer?"

Bormann was thinking of his wife, Gerda, and their 10 children, the oldest of whom was 15. Hitler had been fond of Bormann's big brood, since the Nazis always encouraged large families — as long as they were Aryan.

Hitler looked annoyed.

"Your loyalty is to Germany and your Führer,

34

remember! As I told you, arrangements have been made. Gerda and the children will go to Italy. Perhaps someday you will be reunited. If anyone looks for you, they will think of your family first. That is where they will concentrate their search. Disguise yourself. Wear civilian clothes. You look like a German peasant anyway. Get rid of your party badges and decorations. You will be provided with false papers and identification. Do whatever you have to and remain alive. After a while, everyone will think you died in Berlin. They won't be able to identify all the corpses in this city!"

Bormann was not sure he liked the remark about his looks, but he let it go.

"Yes, my Führer!"

Hitler softened, and did something completely uncharacteristic. He grabbed Bormann by the arm.

"Bormann! When you are clear, open the envelope. In addition to a copy of my last will and testament, there are instructions concerning the bible fragment and all the rest."

Hitler's visage now devolved cruelly.

"You will go to Paris. I will smite that Babylon from the grave!"

"I don't understand, my Führer."

"Listen, Bormann, and listen carefully. There is only one left. The Americans bombed Orhdruf. Destroyed the other two. Killed most of the scientists. Fortunately, one device had already been moved. I was torn. Use it against Zhukov in the East? Perhaps Patton in the West? I ran out of time. But then I had another brilliant idea."

Bormann's mind raced. Too many of Hitler's

brilliant ideas had led them to this pass.

The conversation was surreal. *Götterdämmerung* blaring on the Victrola. Shells bursting overhead. An envelope with secret instructions. One device left? What device?

Was the Führer indeed mad, as some people thought?

What the hell is the Fuhrer talking about? What had he planned to use against Zhukov or Patton?

And Paris?

How the hell can I get to Paris?

CHAPTER 6 - TIGER TANK

On April 30, 1945 Hitler said farewell to his remaining staff. He gave a gentlemanly kiss on the cheek to his female secretaries, all of whom were crying. Then he gave a manly handshake to his male adjutants. The last of whom was Martin Bormann.

He held Bormann's hand a moment longer than the others and stared at him. Many observers had noted that the dictator's clear blue eyes had a mesmerizing effect. They had dulled in recent weeks, but now blazed with their old fanaticism.

"Remember what I told you, Bormann!"

"Jawohl, mein Führer!"

A short while later, at 3:30 PM, Hitler and his new wife retired to his personal quarters. He shot himself. Eva Bruan took cyanide. Their bodies were taken outside the bunker, doused in petrol and burned.

***

With Hitler dead, and his chief henchmen on the run, the Third Reich was on life support. The survivors in the bunker emptied out the bunker's wine cellar, which was remarkably well-stocked considering that Hitler was a teetotaler. Most were soon drunk.

Bormann was not one of them. He would have also been on the run, but his presumptive savior, "Hauptmann Amann", was nowhere to be found.

Whenever he asked about him, or the "arrangements" Hitler had promised, the others in the bunker looked at him as if he were crazy. Some assumed he was also drunk.

"It's every man for himself now, Bormann," one

very inebriated SS Sturmbannführer told him.

Bormann went up to the courtyard several times, only to be driven back underground by Soviet shelling.

Finally, at around 6 PM, when he was on the verge of risking a lone escape, a tall, blond captain sought him out.

"Herr Bormann, I am Hauptman Fritz Amann. You are to come with me."

Bormann could have kissed the strapping Wehrmacht officer.

"Where are we going, Amann?"

"My orders are to head west to Nauen, where we will be met by remnants of Wenck's Army. They will take you as far as Stendahl in Saxony. That is all I know."

That is all you need to know, Bormann thought. Hitler's instructions had been specific. The small, nondescript farm outside Stendahl was off the beaten path, virtually untouched by the war. It was home to a farm family whose discretion was paid for by the promise of a Swiss bank account they could access after the war. Bormann would be provided with new papers and a new identity as a simple farm worker. It would not be the life he was used to, but it would be life. At some point, after all this had blown over, he would find a way to be reunited with his family.

Bormann did not know what was in the envelope Hitler had entrusted to him, but he did know he was not going to Paris. Ever. He had heard rumors that some high-ranking officers had contacts in the Vatican and were even now planning to go to South America. He would seek the Vatican's help. This was ironic, given that he was a committed atheist and church persecutor.

Hauptmann Amann led Bormann to the corridor just inside the door leading up a flight of stairs to the rear entrance of the Führerbunker in the garden of the Reich Chancellery. Lining both walls of the corridor were six soldiers. The men were small. They held an assortment of weapons, most too big for them. One was lugging a Panzerfaust, the inexpensive pre-loaded tube that fired a warhead that could knock out a tank.

Bormann suddenly realized that they were not men, but boys.

"This is my escort! Children!"

Before Amann could reply, the arm of one of the boys shot out in the Nazi salute.

"Heil Hitler. We would die for the Fuhrer!"

Bormann's heart sank. Hitler Youth. Some of them were as fanatical as the SS.

Amann noted the consternation on Bormann's face.

"Don't worry, Herr Bormann," he said. "These are good boys. Proven in battle. They will get you through."

Bormann wondered if Amann had told them that Adolf Hitler was dead and his burned corpse was probably strewn about the courtyard garden thanks to Russian shells. He decided not to ask. He knew that the official announcement, by Grand-Admiral Karl Donitz, the man Hitler named as his successor, would not come until the next day.

"Heil Hitler," he replied with as much effort as he could muster, and saluted.

Amann handed Bormann a well-worn wallet.

"Your new papers are in there."

Bormann wondered what his new name would be. But he did not bother to open the wallet and check. The papers would only prove useful when he was safely in Saxony. If he was caught before he had a chance to hide the envelope from Hitler somewhere on the farm in Stendahl, his new identity wouldn't do him any good.

"Let's go," Amann said. "There is a lull in the shelling. It won't last long. Rolf knows the way."

The boy who had snapped off the salute, stepped forward.

"I'm Rolf, sir."

Handsome lad, Bormann thought. A future blond God when he grew up.

If he grew up.

***

The small band, with Rolf in the lead and Amann and Bormann in the rear, raced across the courtyard, passing a cone-shaped structure that provided ventilation for the bunker. They soon went underground in a U-Bahn tunnel, emerging at the Friedrichstrasse station, adjacent to the Spree river.

They spotted a Tiger tank on the Weidendammer Bridge as it edged its way cautiously across the span.

"The Tiger can give us cover," Amann said.

"It will also draw fire," Bormann replied nervously.

It seemed like the Red Army and Berlin's defenders were shooting from every direction. The noise of battle was deafening.

"What choice do we have? We must get to the

other side of the Spree."

Three of the boys were cut down by machine gun fire as they raced to the tank. No one stopped to help them, although one was crying out for his mother.

Amann grabbed the phone attached to the rear of the tank. He told the crew what they were doing. The tank fired a round at a block of buildings to its front on the far end of the bridge. Then it rumbled ahead, with the survivors of the group walking hunched down behind it.

Just before reaching the far end, disaster struck, in the form of accurate Soviet artillery, which destroyed the tank and killed its crew, whose screams as they burned to death could even be heard over the din of battle.

Two of the remaining boys were killed instantly. Bormann and Amann were knocked to the ground but unhurt. The firing died down and they, and Rolf, the only surviving boy, made it across the bridge. They walked along some railway tracks to Lehrter station.

Amann told Rolf to reconnoiter ahead while they rested. Rolf did so, but soon ran into a Red Army patrol. He hid behind a wrecked railway car while the soldiers passed him. After a few minutes, he heard shots.

When he managed to return to Lehrter station, he found Amann and Bormann. Both had been shot dead and were lying on their backs. Bormann's face had been partly obliterated. Their boots had been stripped off, and they were missing some fingers, where rings probably had been too tight to quickly remove. Their watches and wallets were also undoubtedly gone.

But they seemed otherwise untouched. Red Army

soldiers had plenty of pickings to choose from in the devastated city. In safer places. They did not want to linger too long in what was still a hot combat zone.

Rolf wanted to quit the area, too. But he noticed something sticking part way out of Bormann's jacket pocket. One of his killers probably had started to remove it but didn't finish when he saw it only contained papers. Rolf might have been a Hitler Youth true believer, but he was also a 14-year-old boy. And curious. He pulled the yellow envelope all the way out.

His eyes widened when he saw Hitler's initials.

CHAPTER 7 - HOMECOMING

Young as he was, Rolf Nessing instinctively knew that if the Führer entrusted the envelope to Bormann it must contain something important. But what? And to whom was it directed? His orders, vaguely given by the now-dead Amann, were to get Bormann out of Berlin and head west.

Rolf Nessing thought about leaving the envelope behind. If the Russians caught him with it, they would surely shoot him as a spy, or a messenger. But the reason he was chosen to lead Bormann to safety was that he knew Berlin like the back of his hand, having been born and raised in the small village of Velten, about 15 miles north of Berlin proper.

Rolf made up his mind.

Bormann was wearing civilian clothes. Rolf ripped off his own ill-fitting uniform, and then stripped Bormann, who was not much taller than he was. There were several bloody bullet holes in the man's jacket and trousers. The Russians were apparently lousy shots. Using his fingers, Rolf widened the holes and put on the dead man's clothes.

Bormann was a lot heavier, so the clothes sagged on Rolf, which further increased what he hoped was a disguise that might save his life. With the rents in the clothes, and a face dirtied by, among other things, the explosion of the tank on the bridge, Rolf Essing looked like a ragamuffin, of which there was no shortage in beleaguered Berlin.

He folded the envelope and put it down the back of his underwear. Then he remembered the rumors about what sex-crazed Russian soldiers did to young boys they captured. He switched the envelope to the front. If his underpants were yanked down the papers might go unnoticed.

Rolf left the two corpses where they lay. A German officer and a civilian, apparently victims of war. There was a small fire burning in what was left of a small building nearby and he threw his own I.D. papers into the flames. With any luck, he could pass as just another homeless Berlin orphan.

It was getting dark, and Rolf was very tired. He decided to hole up in another damaged building until dawn. With all the firing and explosions, he doubted he would get much rest. So, he was very surprised when he woke with start. Someone was kicking his leg and shouting at him.

"Raus! Raus!"

It was a Red Army soldier. Others stood around, smiling.

Rolf stood up, and expected the worst.

They frisked him, going through every pocket. But they didn't touch his underclothes, and he almost peed in fright. That wouldn't do the envelope any good, the boy thought wildly. Satisfied that he was just a kid and not a threat, the soldiers laughed and slapped him around a bit. Then, they booted him out of the building, apparently intending to use the space themselves.

Relieved, Rolf headed to Velten, where he hoped his widowed mother and sisters were still alive. His father had died a hero fighting on the Eastern Front in 1943.

Every time the boy spotted a Russian patrol, he quickly found the nearest garbage can and pretended to be scraping it for food. Once a patrol stopped and a Red Army soldier pulled out his bayonet and strode toward him. Rolf again thought the game was up. But the soldier merely placed a can on the ground and punctured it at one corner with the bayonet. He handed it to Rolf and then ran after his comrades who had already begun to move on.

Rolf looked at the partially opened can. It said "Spam". In smaller print: "Made in the U.S.A.", "Hormel" and "Minnesota".

So, this was the Lend Lease processed-pork food the Russians were so fond of. Water was not a problem for Rolf. There were broken pipes everywhere. But the boy's stomach rumbled at the thought of what was in the small tin. He ripped the rest of the metal cover back and tore out the reddish "meat", which earlier in the war the sausage-loving Germans had derided.

He would remember it as one of the best meals he'd ever had.

***

The further Rolf got from the center of the city, the easier the going. The roar of battle lessened until it sounded like thunder in the distance. As he neared Velten, he grew hopeful. The damage in the neighborhoods he passed through went from moderate to slight. When he reached his town's main square, he was relieved to see that it appeared untouched by bombs! There were actually people on the street. Most of them were scrounging, but at least they were out in the open. No one said anything to him. They merely scurried past.

Rolf Essing had been one of the last groups of the

very young or very old Volkssturm conscripts the frantic Nazi regime had drafted to fight its last-ditch battle with the Russians. That was a month ago. His mother, already a war widow, had begged him not to go. But Rolf had been well-indoctrinated by the state, and was eager to show his mettle. And he had, disabling a Soviet tank with a Panzerfaust before being assigned to the Führerbunker.

He reached the street where he lived. With mounting trepidation, he approached his house, a small cottage. He knew the Red Army basically raped its way through eastern Germany prior to surrounding Berlin. He did not see any soldiers, but he feared that they might have already passed through the area.

He would be the man of the house now, and seethed at the thought that his mother and sisters had been defiled by filthy Russians.

There was an old woman sweeping the sidewalk in front of his home. The woman was wearing a tattered dress and old boots, and had a bandanna around her hair. Rolf was about to ask her about his family when she turned at his approach.

"Rolf!"

It was his mother, looking 10 years older than when he left only four weeks earlier. Forgetting his Hitler Youth bearing, he flung himself in her arms and began sobbing.

***

An hour later, Rolf was sitting in the kitchen, being doted on by his mother and two older sisters, Sigrid and Ursula. There was not much food, but what there was, he got.

Miraculously, the women had all escaped the

predations of the Russian Army.

"Some soldiers had some ideas," his mother said delicately, "but one of their officers, a young lieutenant, told them to move on. He said I reminded him of his own mother. He was more cultured than most, I suppose. Anyway, the only Reds we see now are military police and they leave us alone."

Rolf thought of the Russian who gave him the tin of Spam. His family was very lucky.

He told them an abbreviated version of his adventures with Bormann, leaving out the part about the envelope.

"Well, he didn't outlive Hitler by very long," Sigrid said.

"What do you mean?'

"Don't you know, Rolf? The Führer died fighting the Russians yesterday. We heard it on the radio. You must have escaped just in time, thank God."

"Yesterday?"

"Yes," Orsula said. "Admiral Dönitz is now running things."

"Not for much longer," his mother said. "There is nothing left to run."

Rolf was not surprised to hear that Hitler was dead. But now he wondered what he should do with the envelope. His family's luck might run out if it was discovered.

That night, he put the envelope in a tin that in better days had contained an assortment of Danish butter cookies, long since consumed. He buried the tin in the small garden behind his house.

He would open it, and the envelope, when things settled down.

***

Rolf Essing never opened the tin. After the war, Germany was partitioned by the Allies and Velten wound up in East Germany. When he was 17, to help support his family, he joined the Nationale Volksarmee, as the East German army was called. He spent his first tour doing reconstruction work far from home.

When he finally returned to Velten, he discovered that his cottage home, and all like it for a mile around, had been bulldozed to make way for large and drab Soviet-style apartment buildings. His mother and sisters, having initially moved in with relatives, now occupied a seventh-floor apartment in one of the buildings. It was a two-bedroom flat, a rare perquisite given the family because Rolf was now a loyal soldier of the German Democratic Republic.

Rolf Essing's mother died in 1985. Rolf became an engineer and married. He and his wife moved to an apartment in Rheinsberg, where they raised two children. Rolf kept in touch with his sisters, who also married and started their own families. They had traded the family's original two-bedroom apartment to one-bedroom flats in the same building.

After Germany was reunified in 1990, Rolf Essing emigrated to Australia, and was soon joined by his sisters and their families.

In the construction boom that followed the reunification, hundreds of the Soviet-era buildings were demolished. The Essing's old apartment building in Velten was torn down, and new housing that included a popular new hotel was built on the site.

In time, Rolf barely remembered the tin containing Hitler's message, now buried under tons of old and new concrete.

In it were a copy of Adolf Hitler's last will and testament, and half of a page of Old Testament:

Und Zimt und Gerüche und Salben und Weihrauch und Wein und Öl und feines Mehl und Weizen und Tiere und Schafe und Pferde und Wagen und Sklaven und Menschenseelen.

Und die Früchte, nach denen deine Seele begehrte, sind von dir abgewichen, und alles, was zierlich und gut war, ist von dir abgewichen, und du wirst sie überhaupt nicht mehr finden.

Die Kaufleute dieser Dinge, die von ihr reich gemacht wurden, werden aus Furcht vor ihrer Qual, Tränen und Wehklagen stehen.

Und sprach: Ach, leider, diese große Stadt, die mit feinem Leinen und Purpur und Scharlachrot bekleidet und mit Gold und Edelsteinen und Perlen geschmückt ist!

Denn in einer Stunde ist so großer Reichtum zunichte geworden. Und jeder Schiffsführer und die ganze Gesellschaft in Schiffen und Matrosen und so viele, wie der Handel auf dem Seeweg, stand fern,

Und sie weinten, als sie den Rauch ihrer Verbrennung sahen und sagten: Wie ist diese Stadt dieser großen Stadt?

Und sie warfen Staub auf ihren Kopf und weinten und weinten und jammerten und sagten: Leider, diese große Stadt, in der alle, die Schiffe im Meer hatten, wegen ihrer Kostbarkeit reich wurden! denn in einer Stunde ist sie verwüstet.

Freue dich über sie, du Himmel und die heiligen Apostel und Propheten; denn Gott hat dich an ihr gerächt.

Und ein mächtiger Engel nahm einen Stein wie einen großen Mühlstein auf und warf ihn ins Meer und sagte: So wird diese große Stadt Babylon mit Gewalt niedergeworfen und überhaupt nicht mehr gefunden werden.

Und die Stimme der Harper, der Musiker und der Pfeifer und der Trompeter wird in dir gar nicht mehr zu hören sein; und kein Handwerker, von welchem Handwerk auch immer er ist, wird noch mehr in dir gefunden werden; und der Klang eines Mühlsteins wird in dir gar nicht mehr zu hören sein;

Und das Licht einer Kerze soll in dir gar nicht mehr leuchten; und die Stimme des Bräutigams und der Braut wird in dir überhaupt nicht mehr gehört werden; denn deine Kaufleute waren die großen Männer der Erde; denn durch deine Zauberkünste wurden alle Nationen getäuscht.

Und in ihr fand sich das Blut der Propheten und der Heiligen und aller auf Erden Erschlagenen.

The envelope would never see the light of day, unless it was found by some future archaeologist.

CHAPTER 8 - THE 'ONE LEFT'

At about the same time Rolf Essing was burying the envelope in war-torn Berlin, six grumbling workers in Paris were moving a large wooden shipping crate into the back of a storeroom in the Louvre.

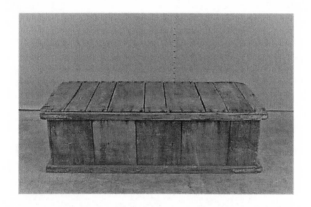

It had been eight months since Paris had been liberated and things were slowly returning to normal. The workers were making more room for returning masterpieces that French authorities had moved from the museum beginning in 1938, as a European war loomed on the horizon.

Most of the museum's greatest works, including massive sculptures, had been sent to châteaux in serene locations in the countryside, far from possible bombing targets. The French were also hopeful that much of the art looted by the Nazis, particularly Herman Goering, would eventually find its way back to the Louvre. During the war, the Nazis plundered private collections belonging to Jewish families or art dealers.

While the victorious Nazis had reopened the Louvre in September 1940, it was virtually empty. But the French were now renovating the museum and opening it gradually to the public. Many of the returned masterpieces were none the worse for wear. Which was amazing. The Mona Lisa, for one, had been moved five times during the war.

The grumbling workers had helped unload both the *Venus de Milo* and the *Winged Victory of Samothrace,* but this crate was easily the largest the workers had seen. It was unmarked, and very heavy.

At one point it slipped off a dolly and almost tilted over.

The man supervising them roundly cursed them.

"Idiots! Be careful!"

"What are you worried about, Martin" one of the workers said. "You look like you've seen a ghost. It's probably just full of Boche statues. You hate the fucking Germans."

"Of course! Of course! I just have a headache. Sorry."

"You should stop drinking cheap wine," one of the men said, and they all laughed.

Then, amid a few Gallic shrugs and much more complaining, which as Frenchmen they saw as their prerogative, the crew managed to muscle the crate, now on two dollies, against a rear wall.

"Satisfied," one of the other men chided their supervisor. "We're going to lunch."

The supervisor, an assistant curator named Martin Bucer, watched the men saunter off. He took out a handkerchief and mopped his brow. He had almost given himself away!

Bucer had been secretly working with the Nazis for years. He had betrayed many Resistance fighters who had come to him for help, never thinking that the long-term caretaker at the Louvre, one who loudly lamented the German occupation to the point where the Gestapo frequently pulled him in, was a collaborator.

***

The contents of the crate had been assembled in great secrecy in July 1944 and trucked, on Adolf Hitler's direct orders, by a contingent of picked troops from the Führerbegleitbrigade to the Louvre in the first week of August.

The Berlin-based Führerbegleitbrigade was tasked with protecting Hitler and proved its loyalty after June 22, 1944 when its leader, Colonel Otto Ernst Remer, arrested the men who had plotted to overthrow the Nazis. The soldiers knew nothing of their cargo, but were determined to get it to Paris.

It was a near-run thing for the small convoy. The Germans were aided by dissent among the Allies. General Charles De Gaulle, anxious that Free French soldiers liberate their capital so that France could claim a place at the peace table wanted to rush into the city. The American Commander, General Dwight D. Eisenhower, was afraid that the Germans would destroy the city and its cultural treasures. While the Allied leaders dithered, their advance toward the French capital stalled.

That allowed the Germans to deliver the crate to Martin Bucer, who made a big show of refusing to accept it, loudly cursing the Nazis for all to hear. That got him another planned trip to Gestapo headquarters, where the Führerbegleitbrigade officer in charge of the crate's delivery gave the collaborator an envelope.

"What's in it?"

"Your instructions, I presume."

"I know that. I mean, what's in the crate?"

The German shrugged. He suspected that its contents were not artistic, but he had strict orders not to open the crate. And he always followed orders.

"What am I supposed to do with it?"

"Why don't you just read the instructions."

Bucer ripped open the envelope. There were three pieces of paper. One appeared to be a fragment of a page from a book.

"Looks like it is from a bible," the German officer said.

Bucer came from Alsace, a region in north-eastern France that borders Switzerland and Germany. His family was primarily German, and he was an early convert to Naziism, and first recruited by the Abwehr, the German military intelligence service of the Wehrmacht. Later, he became an important Gestapo agent.

Bucer did not consider himself a collaborator. He had spent so many years pretending to be a loyal Frenchman that his German was a bit rusty. He struggled to translate the archaically written and boldly typed Old-Testament fragment:

Und nach diesen Dingen sah ich einen anderen Engel vom Himmel herabkommen, der große Macht hatte; und die Erde wurde mit seiner Herrlichkeit erleuchtet.

Und er schrie mit starker Stimme und sagte: Babylon, der Große, ist gefallen, ist gefallen und wird zur Behausung von Teufeln und zum Griff eines jeden üblen Geistes und zu einem Käfig für jeden unreinen und verhassten Vogel.

Denn alle Nationen haben vom Wein des Zorns ihrer Unzucht getrunken, und die Könige der Erde haben Unzucht mit ihr begangen, und die Kaufleute der Erde werden durch die Fülle ihrer Delikatessen reich.

Und ich hörte eine andere Stimme vom Himmel und sagte: Komm aus ihr, mein Volk, dass du nicht an ihren Sünden teilnimmst und dass du nicht von ihren Plagen empfängst.

Denn ihre Sünden haben den Himmel erreicht, und Gott hat an ihre Missetaten gedacht.

Belohnung sie, wie sie dich belohnt, und verdopple sie nach ihren Werken: in dem Becher, den sie zu ihrem Doppel gefüllt hat.

Wie sehr sie sich selbst verherrlicht und köstlich gelebt hat, so viel Qual und Leid schenke sie: denn sie spricht in ihrem Herzen: Ich sitze eine Königin und bin keine Witwe und werde keinen Kummer sehen.

Darum werden ihre Plagen eines Tages kommen, Tod und Trauer und Hunger; und sie wird völlig mit Feuer verbrannt werden; denn stark ist der Herrgott, der sie richtet.

Und die Könige der Erde, die Unzucht begangen und köstlich mit ihr gelebt haben, werden sie beklagen und für sie klagen, wenn sie den Rauch ihres Verbrennens sehen werden,

Sie standen aus Furcht vor ihrer Qual in der

Ferne und sagten: Leider, diese große Stadt Babylon, diese mächtige Stadt! denn in einer Stunde ist dein Gericht gekommen.

Und die Kaufleute der Erde werden über sie weinen und trauern; denn niemand kauft seine Waren mehr:

Die Waren aus Gold und Silber und Edelsteinen und aus Perlen und feinem Leinen und Purpur und Seide und Scharlach und allem Thymianholz und allen Gefäßen aus Elfenbein und allen Gefäßen aus edelstem Holz, und aus Messing und Eisen und Marmor

"Give me that," the German officer said, impatiently. He read:

"And cinnamon, and odours, and ointments, and frankincense, and wine, and oil, and fine flour, and wheat, and beasts, and sheep, and horses, and chariots, and slaves, and souls of men.

And the fruits that thy soul lusted after are departed from thee, and all things which were dainty and goodly are departed from thee, and thou shalt find them no more at all.

The merchants of these things, which were made rich by her, shall stand afar off for the fear of her torment, weeping and wailing,

And saying, Alas, alas, that great city, that was clothed in fine linen, and purple, and scarlet, and decked with gold, and precious stones, and pearls!

For in one hour so great riches is come to nought. And every shipmaster, and all the company in ships, and sailors, and as many as trade by sea, stood afar off,

And cried when they saw the smoke of her burning, saying, what city is like unto this great city!

And they cast dust on their heads, and cried, weeping and wailing, saying, Alas, alas, that great city, wherein were made rich all that had ships in the sea by reason of her costliness! for in one hour is she made desolate.

Rejoice over her, thou heaven, and ye holy apostles and prophets; for God hath avenged you on her.

And a mighty angel took up a stone like a great millstone, and cast it into the sea, saying, thus with violence shall that great city Babylon be thrown down, and shall be found no more at all.

And the voice of harpers, and musicians, and of pipers, and trumpeters, shall be heard no more at all in thee; and no craftsman, of whatsoever craft he be, shall be found any more in thee; and the sound of a millstone shall be heard no more at all in thee;

And the light of a candle shall shine no more at all in thee; and the voice of the bridegroom and of the bride shall be heard no more at all in thee: for thy merchants were the great men of the earth; for by thy sorceries were all nations deceived.

And in her was found the blood of prophets, and of saints, and of all that were slain upon the earth."

The officer looked up.

"What the hell does it mean?"

"I don't know," Bucer replied.

The other two pages were in high-school-level French. The top page contained an order, with his name on it! It instructed Bucer not to do anything until he received the matching bottom half of the Bible fragment, which would authenticate the material. The second page, also with his name, was a set of specific technical instructions.

As Bucer started to read it, his eyes widened in shock. So, that was it! Some sort of bomb!

Bucer could feel, rather than see, the German officer trying to peer at the document. He didn't know if the man could read French, so he moved away.

"This is for me only," Bucer said, sharply. "Direct from the Führer himself!"

The officer shrugged and lighted a foul-smelling cigarette.

"Very mysterious," he said. "Cloak-and-dagger stuff. But the Führer must know what he is doing. Personally, I don't trust you Frogs."

Bucer ignored the insult. He could hardly believe what he was reading. What good would a single bomb do at this stage of the war?

Finally, he folded all the papers into the envelope and put it in his pocket.

"Take me back to my apartment!"

"Not the Louvre?"

"No! And I want you and your men to escort me to my door."

Bucer was taking no chances that anyone might see the envelop before he hid it. As long as it was on his person, it might have well been his death warrant. Hitler had obviously wanted to ensure his loyalty by putting his name on the instructions.

"Yes, sir," the German said, sarcastically. "But

then we must make this all look realistic, no?"

"What do you mean?"

The officer punched Bucer in the face. Several times. Bucer fell. He got off the floor, spitting blood. One of his teeth felt loose. His jaw was already swelling and he knew he would have a black eye, maybe two.

The German was kneading his knuckles and smiling.

"That should do it," the Führerbegleitbrigade officer said, happily.

"The Gestapo never roughed me up," Bucer complained.

"Much the pity."

The officer, a veteran of the Eastern Front, considered himself a "real" soldier.

He despised collaborators.

He punched Bucer again, harder.

CHAPTER 9 - OLD COMRADES

Eisenhower had been right to be concerned about the fate of Paris as Allied armies approached the French capital in the late summer of 1944.

It was Adolf Hitler's long-standing order to General Dietrich von Choltitz, the commander of the German garrison in Paris, to level the city if it was in danger of falling to the Allies.

Choltitz was shocked. A cultured man, he had come to love the city, and by this time in the war he was sure Hitler was insane. He defied the order and surrendered on August 25.

That same day, major units of the 2nd French Armored Division and US 4th Infantry Division liberated the city amid an uprising by its populace.

Once Paris was secure, the French began to deal with collaborators. Women who had slept with, and in many cases loved, German soldiers had their hair shorn off. They were lucky. Many male collaborators were roughly handled; some were summarily executed.

Martin Bucer was not one of them. In fact, his wartime "heroism" made him something of a celebrity in post-war Paris. In 1946, he was promoted and made a full curator at the Louvre. He even lectured about his Resistance exploits at the Sorbonne. And for the first time in his life, despite his rather dumpy looks, he was found attractive by some young women students.

He realized that with Germany defeated and divided, his previous slavish loyalty to Nazism made no sense. Nor did holding on to the contents of the envelope he'd received when the Nazis delivered the crate the previous year. The second half of the Bible passage would never arrive. So, right after Germany surrendered, Bucer retrieved the envelope from under the floorboard in his apartment where it was hidden.

Just knowing it existed and would be his death warrant if discovered had given him nightmares.

He started to burn all the material. But when he came to the Bible passage, he hesitated. There was nothing in it that would link it to him. He replaced it in the envelope that had Adolf Hitler's embossed initials and put it back in its hiding place.

An idea had formed in his head.

Bucer doubted anyone would blame him for accepting the crate from the Germans. After all, his protestations had been loud when he was dragged away by the Gestapo. And when he left its headquarters at 4 Avenue Foch in the 16th Arrondissement, his face had been mashed up, thanks to that pig of a German officer!

***

"Martin, what are you thinking about?"

Bucer was sitting up in bed, smoking a Caporal cigarette, next to one of his students, a young girl named Lisette Moreau.

"The war, my dear. The war."

It was a line that worked wonders, although he hoped it did not work too well right away. He was exhausted. They had made love all afternoon. Lisette was his favorite bedmate. Vigorous to a fault. Had the French Army showed such verve in 1940, he thought, France might have won the war.

"I think you must put it behind you, Martin."

Bucer, who had been called up by his Alsatian reserve regiment, had surrendered during an ill-conceived probe of German lines during the "Phony War" that preceded the German invasion of France in May of 1940. He had been repatriated by his captors after France surrendered "for health reasons", while many of his comrades went into prison camps, or worse. His "health" improved quite remarkably and he found a position in the Louvre, and was soon doing the bidding of his Nazi masters.

"Easier said than done, I'm afraid."

Bucer sighed, for effect.

"Yes. I know," the girl said. "My father has the same trouble."

That reminded her of something. She looked at her watch, which was the only thing she was wearing.

"Oh. I'm late. Do you mind? I have to run."

Bucer tried to look disappointed.

"But it is my day off."

The silly girl looked bereft.

"It is just that one of my father's old comrades is coming to dinner. I want to help my mother. It is a special occasion."

"In that case, of course I don't mind," Bucer said, much relieved. He patted her delicious bottom as she got out of bed. "Old comrades are important."

***

That evening, in their small apartment near the Eiffel Tower, Lisette and her mother, Noel, were serving dinner to Armand Moreau and his wartime comrade, a man named Blaise Allard. The men, private soldiers, had mustered into the same French regiment and were captured together in the 1940 debacle.

Since both men had been postal workers in civilian life before being called up as reservists, the Germans, anxious to restore order in Occupied France, allowed them to resume their former jobs. Both postmen were ideally placed to aid the Resistance when it formed, and they did.

But Allard was arrested in July of 1944 by the Gestapo and brutally tortured. He never implicated his friend, Armand. In fact, he never implicated anyone. The Gestapo, with the Allies moving closer to Paris, had other things to worry about, so they shipped him to Natzweiler-Struthof, a concentration camp located in the Vosges Mountains near the German border.

The camp specialized in working members of the French Resistance to death. As Allied armies overran all of France, the Nazis began to execute many of the survivors. A small staff of SS personnel was finishing this grisly work when the camp was liberated by the French First Army on 23 November 1944.

The outraged French soldiers killed the SS guards and cared as best they could for the few surviving inmates. Many died.

But a gaunt and half-crazed Blaise Allard survived.

Allard's mind had been somewhat repaired, but his physical strength never recovered. He had lost all his teeth and, even with government-supplied dentures, had trouble eating. He apologized profusely as he barely picked at the wonderful coq au vin that the Moreau women had prepared for him. But the wine was excellent, and for dessert he did have two helpings of the delicious crème brûlée, which gave him no trouble.

Everyone avoided talking about the war. That was fine with Allard. It was nice to be with a friend and his family. Allard had not married. He would never have children of his own, thanks to unmentionable injuries suffered at the hands of the Nazis in Natzweiler-Struthof. But at least he was alive, unlike most of the other inmates at the camp.

The conversation turned to Lisette. She was indeed a beauty, as Allard remarked, knowing it would please Armand.

"What are you doing now, Lisette. Modeling? Starring in the cinema?"

They all laughed.

"No, I am in school. The Sorbonne. Studying art. I have the most wonderful teachers. One of them is a curator at the Louvre."

"Oh, please, Lisette, let's not hear more about Bucer," Noel Moreau said.

She turned to Allard.

"She has a crush on the man."

Allard had a very strange look on his face.

"Lisette, did you say, Bucer? Martin Bucer?"

"Yes. Why? Did you know him in the Resistance?"

"Lisette, no war talk," her mother chided.

"No, it's all right, Noel. I don't mind. I'm just surprised he is still alive."

"Oh, yes," Lisette gushed. "Mr. Bucer is alive. The Gestapo never got him."

That did not surprise Blaise Allard. But he had been sure the Resistance would have.

***

After dinner, Allard, claiming that he was feeling a bit weak, asked if Armand Moreau would walk him home.

"Why don't you just stay here for the night?" Noel Moreau asked.

"Oh, no. Thank you. I will be fine. I don't live far."

"The walk will do you good, Armand" Noel said.

They were barely out the door when Armand said, "What do you want to tell me, Blaise?"

"You don't miss much, my friend."

"That's how I stayed alive during the war. What is it? Your whole demeanor changed when Lisette mentioned Bucer."

"He is a traitor. He is the one who betrayed me."

"Bucer!"

Armand Moreau stopped walking and stared at his friend. He fumbled for a cigarette and lit it with a shaking hand.

"Yes, Martin Bucer. It was a message I gave to Bucer that the Gestapo used against me. They actually showed me the message. They could only have gotten it from him. And I met two other men in Natzweiler he betrayed. The SS killed them the day before I was scheduled to die. I'm sure that bastard thinks that I am also dead. Did you ever wonder why your group was never touched, while my unit was rolled up by the Gestapo?"

"I thought we were just lucky, Blaise. I always felt guilty about it."

"It was because you never had to pass messages through Bucer! He was not on your route. We did,

65

and I am the only one of my unit to still be alive. He got all the others killed!"

"What can we do? Bucer is a war hero to many, and a respected curator."

Allard smiled, grimly.

"I may not be much anymore, Armand. But I still have some contacts in the Resistance. I am a bit of a celebrity to them. One of the few to make it out of the Natzweiler hellhole alive. They will be very interested in Martin Bucer."

Blaise Allard put his hand on Armand Moreau's shoulder.

"Are you with us, my friend?"

Armand Moreau thought about his beautiful daughter. He smiled grimly.

"With pleasure."

CHAPTER 10 - RETRIBUTION

The guard at the Louvre Palace, the main building where the crate was stored, greeted Bucer.

"Isn't this your day off, Monsieur?"

"I forgot to do something, Louis."

"That is what I call dedication, sir."

Idiot, Bucer thought.

When he got to the storeroom, it was deserted. The room was only dimly lighted, but he knew approximately where the crate had wound up, and found it soon enough against the back wall. Other, smaller crates had been stacked atop it.

A small ladder leaned against the wall, and there was a work table nearby, with various tools and a large flashlight.

Even though they were smaller, some of the other crates were heavy. Bucer entertained the thought of just dropping them down to the floor, but he knew that might attract attention. Or they might spill open, and how would he explain that? So, he would have to muscle the crates down individually himself. It would take time, but he had to make sure there was nothing in the crate that could incriminate him!

Bucer dragged the ladder over. He took off his jacket, draping it over a dolly. Then he walked to the front of the storeroom and locked the door. When he returned to the crate, he positioned the torch so that his workspace was well-illuminated.

It took Bucer just over an hour to uncover the big crate. He was sweating heavily. He had run out of curses, French and German.

The crate was sealed. Bucer took a pry bar from

the workbench and levered the top cover off. What he now saw astounded him.

It certainly did not look like any bomb he'd ever seen. He remembered yelling at the work crew when they dropped it. That was probably an overreaction, which he'd laughed off at the time to deflect suspicion. The Nazis were careful with ordinance. This contraption wouldn't go off with mere jostling, although it was probably packed with enough high-explosives to bring down the building, if not a city block.

There were two small boxes jutting from the top of the contraption. One in the middle and the other on the end. Bucer got a screwdriver from the workbench and unscrewed the covers on each. He no longer had any interest in the workings of the boxes. His incriminating instructions, now in ashes he'd dumped in a waste bin, would have had him turn some dials on the timers to synchronize them.

Now, all he was interested in was seeing if there was anything in the crate that would link the bomb to him.

He did not expect to find anything, and was relieved when he didn't.

Bucer took the Hitler-embossed envelope from his pocket, folded it neatly, and placed in next to the timer in the middle box. Then he resealed both boxes.

Martin Bucer had no intention of leaving the bomb

in situ. His decision was not altruistic. He had no great love of the French. And for that matter, no real love of art, a strange attitude for a curator. He liked the prestige, privileges, salary and sex his position gave him, but that was all. That did not mean he wanted to walk around a museum where a bomb lay moldering. Some idiot might find it, open the timing boxes and accidentally set it off.

For Bucer was pretty certain that had he followed the original instructions, he would have been blown to bits. He knew from experience that the Nazis were not big on witnesses. They had even assured him that they had eliminated everyone who could attest to his own perfidy. As soon as he turned a dial in one of the boxes, the bomb would have detonated.

But what if he "discovered" the device and warned the authorities? The Hitler envelope and its Biblical script would be a sensation. Bucer's fraudulent heroic status would only be reinforced. He would be a true hero of Paris. More honors and promotions would follow.

Even the Directorship of the Louvre would not be out of reach!

Bucer smiled. He needed witnesses. He went back to work, closing the lid and re-stacking, very carefully, the smaller crates on top of the one containing the bomb.

Tomorrow, he would announce that he wanted to investigate what was stored in this room. The administration would believe Bucer was just being conscientious. He would assemble a small work crew and go through the motions of opening all the crates. He would start in the back. Checking out the oldest

69

crates would only make sense.

But when Bucer reopened the big crate, he would be properly astounded. He would unseal the middle box and "discover" the envelope, with its mysterious scripture passage. He would then perform a rudimentary examination of the cylinder and loudly declare that he thought it was a bomb! Of course, he would supervise intently, to make sure no one else touched the timers. He would order everyone out of the room and tell them to call the military, while he courageously stayed with the cylinder.

The bomb experts would hopefully move the crate to some remote location and disarm the device. Bucer considered telling them his suspicions about the timer being booby-trapped, but decided against it. The less people knew about his knowledge of Nazi tactics the better.

The bomb-disposal people would probably be cautious, anyway.

And if they were careless, well, too bad for them.

***

Bucer stopped for a celebratory brandy on the way back to his flat. By the time he got home, it was near midnight. He was slightly tipsy, and paid little attention to the two men unloading a large rolled-up carpet from the black van idling outside his building. In post-War Paris someone was always moving into an apartment, at all hours.

When Bucer opened the door to his second-floor apartment, there was a man sitting in his favorite armchair, barely lighted by the moon streaming in the window. The man turned on a lamp on the table next to him.

70

"Who the hell are you!"

"Armand Moreau."

"And that is supposed to mean something to me? What are you doing in my apartment? Get out before I call the police!"

"I am Lisette's father."

Oh, Christ, Bucer thought. An outraged father. Just what I need. But what is the problem? Moreau is a Frenchman. His daughter is of age.

The door behind Bucer closed. He turned to see someone else. A gaunt man who looked vaguely familiar walked up to him.

"And I am Blaise Allard. Remember me?"

Recognition dawned on Bucer.

"But they told me you were dead!"

"Never believe a Nazi," Allard said, smiling.

Bucer's gaze drifted down to the long knife in Allard's hand.

"Wait!" he screamed. "There is something I must tell you!"

"Tell it to your Nazi friends in hell, you piece of shit," Allard said and shoved the blade into Bucer, again and again.

***

The disappearance of Martin Bucer, revered curator and Resistance hero, created quite a sensation in Paris. Lisette Moreau was devastated. Her parents were properly sympathetic, even after she told them Bucer had been her lover. Later, of course, her father told his friend Blaise that he wished he had wielded the knife.

An article in *Paris Match* speculated that neo-Nazis were behind Bucer's disappearance and probable murder, apparently taking revenge for his staunch anti-German activities during the war.

That rumor aggravated his real killers in the Resistance. But they nevertheless kept quiet. They had other traitors in their sights, and did not want them looking over their shoulders.

Bucer's corpse was never discovered, although the carpet it had been wrapped in was used several more times, for other collaborators who thought they had avoided French "justice".

But the unmarked crate, which Bucer had planned on "discovering" to great acclaim, also lay undiscovered. It gathered dust, largely forgotten, in the rear of a storeroom that slowly filled with many more crates and boxes.

Inside was Adolf Hitler's final vengeance weapon, with a U-235 core that had a half-life of 700 million years.

The Rache Bombe still threatened not only the Louvre, but all of Paris.

NOW

CHAPTER 11 - BLOODY BLOUSE

The white van, rented of course, lay halfway through the front facade of the bistro on Rue La Fontaine in the 16th Arrondissement.

To get there, it had to first crash through five or six outdoor tables, where people, some Parisians, some foreign tourists, sat having an afternoon coffee and pastry, or perhaps a glass of wine and some cheese.

There was blood and glass everywhere. Emergency workers, by now used to this sort of thing, had covered the dead and had stabilized the living, some of whom were already being loaded on ambulances. Men were cursing, women were crying and police officers were taking statements and, where they could without interfering with the medical people, cordoning off areas of the scene. Other gendarmes, armed with automatic rifles, stood in the street.

Two officers from the elite Groupe d'Intervention de la Gendarmerie (GIGN) unit were looking into the van, whose driver had escaped, unharmed, in the confusion. Described as dark-skinned and "Arabic", he had apparently been wearing his seatbelt.

Five people, two Parisians and three British tourists, were dead. All had been crushed by the van outside the bistro. Seven others were injured; three of them from inside, including a waiter. All the injured were French.

A stroller lay on its side in a puddle of blood.

Fortunately, it was not the blood of the two-year-old who had been in the stroller. The boy, from Great Britain and now an orphan, was only slightly injured. The blood was his mother's.

Only the fact that the child had survived kept Claudette Lebel from losing it. She had carried the strangely quiet boy to an ambulance herself.

She handed him off to an attendant.

"Probably shock," the man said. "We'll take good care of him, Lieutenant."

Although she was in plainclothes, the man recognized her from previous terrorist incidents.

Lebel looked at him. He saw something in her eyes.

"Are you alright?"

"Yes, I'm fine," she replied, and then walked back to the carnage.

***

"You need some time off. Why don't you take a vacation?"

"I don't want a vacation."

Marcel Gerard, the Chief Superintendent of the Paris Homicide Division, knew he couldn't force Claudette Lebel to take time off. She was, after all, one of his finest officers. Moreover, she was the granddaughter of Claude Lebel, the man who had stopped "The Jackal" from assassinating Charles De Gaulle in 1963. And her own father had retired as the Police Commissioner in Marseilles. Her decision to enter the National Gendarmerie had created a media sensation, and Lebel's successes in several high-profile murder cases had burnished her reputation.

It did not hurt her image, particularly among

Frenchmen, that she was also very pretty. Even dressed as usual in a rather severe suit, with her strawberry-blond hair swept back in a simple French twist that highlighted her fine facial bone structure and gray eyes, Claudette Lebel turned heads, both male and female.

They were sitting in Gerard's paneled office in the gleaming new headquarters of the Direction Régionale de Police Judiciaire de Paris at 36 rue du Bastion in the 17th arrondissement. All the functions and departments of the DRPJ were now concentrated in the new building, save for the Brigade de Recherche et d'Intervention, which specialized in armed robbery and kidnappings. The BRI, or "Anti-Gang Brigade" as it was commonly called, remained at 36 quai des Orfèvres, on the same small Seine island, Île de la Cité, occupied by Notre Dame.

The old headquarters was known informally as the "Trente-six". Many wondered if the new locale, which shared the same address number, would absorb the nickname.

Lieutenant Lebel had just reported on the bloody scene at the bistro. Although her presentation was, as usual, coldly professional, she had a slightly haunted look that Gerard knew well. She had gone from one bloody murder scene to another over the past two years, without a break. And now this bistro massacre. In French police terms, Claudette was close to being "brûlé" - burnt out.

"Well, at least take tomorrow off. When you get back, I have another assignment for you."

Claudette Lebel bristled.

"What about this case? I want to catch the bastard

who did it."

"We all do, Claudette. But GIGN has claimed jurisdiction. You know how closed-knit they are. My hands are tied. Go home. Open up some wine. Get a good night's sleep."

It was partly true. Gerard had enough clout to insist that his division also investigate, but he did not want to waste that particular chip just yet. Unfortunately, as he knew, there would be larger tragedies than one with, God help him, just five dead.

Claudette Lebel nodded. She was very tired. A day off would do her good. She stood.

"Claudette."

"Yes."

"Perhaps you can borrow a coat from someone before you leave."

"A coat?"

"Your blouse."

She looked down. Her white blouse had a large bloodstain on it.

"Not the baby's," she said.

***

It was almost 9 PM when Claudette Lebel neared her apartment on the Canal Saint Martin in the 10th Arrondissement. It was a trendy area, popular with young lovers holding hands as they walked along the waterway flanked by older buildings. The area reminded many of Amsterdam. Some locals were playing boules, rolling heavy black balls on a tamped-down sandbank. Claudette had never rolled a ball in her life.

And after her divorce, love was the furthest thing from her mind.

Once in her one-bedroom apartment, she undressed quickly, throwing the bloodied blouse in the trash. She opened a bottle of Bordeaux and poured herself a large glass, which she took into her bathroom. She sat, naked, on the edge of her bidet while her tub filled with hot water. When the bath met her expectations, she slid into the water, placing the wine glass on a window sill. She poured a bath gel onto a sponge and washed herself.

Then, she sipped her wine and soaked for almost an hour, occasionally turning on the hot water tap with her toes.

After drying herself off, she padded, still naked, into the kitchen and filled her glass. Then she went into her bedroom. Before dressing there, she looked at herself in a standing mirror. At 35, she still had good muscle tone, thanks to twice-a-week workouts at the police gym and frequent early-morning runs along the canal. Her breasts, while smallish, did not sag. The hand not holding the wine glass drifted down toward the small patch of dark blond pubic hair, which she kept trimmed, on her pudenda. Her fingers lingered there, not moving. Love might not be in the cards, but she missed sex. It had been just over a year since she and Charles had called it quits after four years of marriage.

Claudette did not blame him. She'd married late, hoping that life with the handsome architect would take the edge off her police work. At first, it had. Charles included her in his artistic devotion, and gave her a new appreciation of the glorious treasures she had often taken for granted.

But it didn't last. She was soon drawn back into

the brutal world of murder and terrorism. She kept police hours, and sometimes did not see him for days at a time. They drifted apart. When a position in his field came up in Rome, they decided to make a clean break.

Thank God, they did not have children.

Since the divorce, Claudette had thrown herself into her job, and avoided romantic entanglements. A few of her colleagues at work, married and not, had made passes at her, which she quickly rebuffed. But there were no recriminations or hard feelings. They were Frenchmen, after all. They would never have thought of insulting such a beautiful woman by ignoring her!

Everyone still liked her, although she knew she was getting a reputation as a "man hater".

Claudette thought of the shocked toddler she had carried at the bistro.

Her fingers left her private parts.

She sighed and took her wine to bed.

CHAPTER 12 - MASON

John Mason was slightly hungover.

The night before, he'd done a modest Manhattan pub crawl with some literary and journalistic friends, including Sebastian Junger. What started out as a celebration of Mason's latest book, now in final galleys at Knopf, had devolved into the trading of war stories fueled by shots of Jameson.

Mason always felt uncomfortable about talking about his experiences, except with this group. They'd seen and done just about everything, all over the globe, and he felt comfortable letting his guard down. Drinking Irish whisky didn't hurt.

Well, perhaps a bit. As his slight headache and sour taste in his mouth and stomach reminded him, Mason was no spring chicken anymore. Now in his mid-30's, with a knee that occasionally ached in cold weather from where some bits of shrapnel had been removed (he'd always thought that was an old-wife's tale), some sunrises weren't as welcome as others. Especially in the middle of a work week.

Mason stopped for a strong black coffee at a trendy coffee shop near his Greenwich Village apartment. He knew the young woman who served him during previous visits. As usual, she flirted with him. He knew he was good-looking, with tousled dark-brown hair, blue eyes and chiseled facial features slightly marred by another small shrapnel-induced scar, unnoticeable when he forgot to shave, which he often did. Just under 6-feet tall and single, Mason did not lack for feminine companionship.

The cute coffee-shop barista was a tad young for

him, so that was as far as the flirting would go. She still tried to slip him a free croissant, but he politely declined. Black coffee was all he was able to manage on the subway trip uptown to *The New York Times*, where he occupied a cubical as a writer in the Arts and Leisure Department in the "Times Tower" skyscraper at 620 Eighth Avenue between West 40th and 41st Streets.

***

Mason exchanged greetings with some nearby cubicle colleagues and powered up his computer. As usual, there were dozens of emails. He read them all, even those from PR flacks. A lot of his colleagues never read PR suggestions or tips. If they got through spam protection, they were quickly ditched. Mason knew bullshit when he saw it. But just because someone had an agenda and was paid to pump a story, didn't mean it wasn't a good idea.

Mason knew he was a bit of an odd duck at the *Times*. Most of the other people in his department had come from the Ivy League and were considered experts in their field. Most had dreamed of winding up at the Times. Not him. When growing up, he dreamed of the Olympics.

Mason had been 19 and on a track scholarship, and just starting his sophomore year at Villanova University, majoring in Art History, when he watched the Twin Towers come down amid the gasps and cries of fellow students in one of the school cafeterias.

He dropped out of Villanova to enlist in the Marines, disappointing his parents, his high school track coach and just about everyone in Lorain, Ohio.

Lorain, a declining Rust Belt city on Lake Erie had few heroes to brag about. The citizens were patriotic, but they expected John Mason, the state champion in the 440, to eventually run his way into the Olympics.

"You're not as fast as a bullet, John," Mike Mazucco, his track coach had told him when he stopped by to say goodbye before boot camp. "Why don't you finish college, at least. Go into R.O.T.C. and get a commission. Villanova has one of the best track programs in the country."

"War will be over by then, Coach."

Of course, it wasn't. And after two tours, and too much combat, he did not reenlist, despite the entreaties of his last company commander at Camp Lejeune, where he had been sent to recuperate behind a desk.

"John, you're the best staff sergeant in the outfit. You're sure to make Gunny next year. And you're a born leader. I can recommend you for O.C.S. if you want. Don't worry about your knee. You won't get stuck doing paperwork forever. With your record, we can finagle things to get you back on the line."

To be polite, Mason told his captain that he'd sure think it over, but when the time came he put in his papers. Getting back "on the line" was what he wanted to avoid. And he knew with his purple hearts and Silver Star, that's where he would be headed. He still loved his country, and was not afraid, but he had no intention of making it a career in a military that was going to be fighting folks all over the globe for the next 20 years. And that was where things were going.

As for him, he wanted to go back to school. When

he wasn't being shot at in Iraq and Afghanistan, he'd been fascinated by the historical treasures he'd seen.

Villanova, of course, took him back, sans the track scholarship, which his bum knee made moot in any case. But the school had been very decent about finding him other types of financial aid, although he did graduate with nearly $40,000 in student loans. To that he added another $20,000 when he continued at Villanova and earned a Master's Degree in Classical Studies.

Both his parents died while he was in graduate school. They had been hard-hit by the loss of manufacturing jobs in Ohio, and most of what they owned, including their modest house, went to pay debts and funeral expenses. As an only child with just a couple of aunts spread across the nation, there was no reason, except for his parents' funerals, a year apart, for Mason ever to return to Lorain.

Both Villanova and the Marine Corps had powerful alumni connections, and Mason was able to get a job in the art department of a small ad agency in Manhattan. There, a woman he dated told him that he should write a book about his experiences as a Marine.

He was reluctant to do that until she suggested he concentrate on the artistic and architectural ruins he'd seen. He did, minimizing his combat experiences and stressing the dangers facing many of the world's cultural treasures. With ISIS and other fanatics destroying monuments and artifacts, Mason's book was nothing if not timely.

Mason discovered he was a facile writer and found an agent who pitched his book to the John Hopkins

University Press in Baltimore, which published it. Eventually titled, *War Among the Ruins*, the book sold modestly and Mason fully expected it to be his only book. But it got noticed by people in Washington, D.C., and several influential writers in New York, such as Junger, championed it. And soon the Knopf Doubleday Publishing Group came calling with a three-book deal.

The money from book writing allowed Mason to move from a small apartment in Brooklyn's DUMBO (down under the Manhattan Bridge Overpass) neighborhood to an even smaller but trendy apartment on Christopher Street in lower Manhattan's Greenwich Village.

Mason knew that his niche books would never be mass-market best sellers, and he wondered what would happen when the money ran out. He thought about teaching at one of the city's universities but then, almost out of nowhere, he found a dream job. The combination of military man and art expert was catnip to *The New York Times*, which offered him a position.

And told him he could continue to write books.

CHAPTER 13 - OYSTERS

Mason's headache was almost gone and his appetite had returned to the point where he thought a ham-and-egg croissant from a nearby Starbucks might just save his life. He was halfway out of his seat when Barry Eliason strolled into his cubicle and plopped down on the corner of his desk.

Eliason was the editor of the Arts and Leisure section at *The New York Times*. Mason settled back down.

"You look like crap," Eliason said.

"And good morning to you, Barry."

Eliason was blond, thin and the picture of healthy living. Despite that, they were good friends. Eliason was also a runner, although he came to the activity later in life, as a way to lose weight. Mason's knee, except for the cold-weather twinges, was not really an impediment, but Mason now restricted himself to five-mile runs around Central Park, or along the West Side Highway, often with Eliason.

Unlike Mason, Eliason was a health nut, and always going on about hummus, fresh vegetables, flax seeds, yogurt and, of course, the dangers of red meat and alcohol. He never passed on a chance to chide Mason about his diet and drinking habits. Mason, who had the metabolism of a hummingbird and never put on weight no matter what he ate, put up with the good-natured kidding. He could leave Eliason in the dust if he wanted to. But his sprinting days were long gone. If no one is shooting at you, why bother?

"Did you forget we are training for a mini-marathon?" Eliason asked. "It's in three weeks, you know."

They had signed up for one in Montauk out on Long island.

"I'm pumped," Mason said. "Can't wait to scarf down some lobster rolls and beer after the race."

Eliason shook his head in resignation.

"I knew there was a reason you wanted to go. Anyway, how is the story on Hudson Yards coming along?"

Hudson Yards was a new ultra-upscale million-square-feet complex that had recently opened on New York's west side. At a $25 billion price tag it was billed as the largest private real-estate development in the history of the United States. Critics labeled it a playground for billionaires; another sign that Manhattan was no place for the middle class. And some people wondered if what was basically a huge shopping mall made any sense in the era of Amazon.

But the project's developers, who received $6 billion in tax breaks from the city, claimed that Hudson Yards, with its office buildings, hotels, residences and performing-arts venues was really "a city within a city". They argued that it could support all the shops and restaurants, drawing people from other boroughs and becoming a mecca for tourists.

"Robert Moses would be proud," Mason said.

He had just re-read *The Power Broker* by Robert A. Caro, and was a bit soured on the "if you build it, they will come" mantra.

"I can't wait until you see my expense report," Mason continued. "I found a restaurant where the oysters were $5 each." He smiled. "I had a dozen.

Research."

"I know. I know. It's a joke. But what about the story."

Mason had been told to do a once-over-lightly piece on the artwork and sculptures that graced some of the Hudson Yard boutiques.

"I think the bivalves cost more than some of the paintings," he said. "Anyway, I'll have it done by the weekend. What's the rush? The paper has a Hudson Yard story just about every day. Got to keep the advertisers happy, I guess."

Mason knew he was one of the most-reliable reporters on the *Times*. He made all his deadlines. In fact, he was usually early, something that did not sit too well with some of his "superstar" colleagues, who took months to craft their gems.

It was unlike Eliason to ask about one of Mason's assignments when it was not due yet.

"No rush. But Fred Adler asked me if you had anything big going."

Adler was the editor who ran the *Times* prestigious Foreign Desk.

"Adler?"

"I think he wants to steal you for something."

"Any idea?"

"Not a clue. But just hear him out. You can always say no. I'll back you up."

That was good to hear. Mason had his fill of overseas work, especially in countries where people were shooting at him or trying to blow him up. And that was par for the course for some foreign correspondents. In fact, only the night before he had chided Junger and his pals for going into war zones unarmed with anything but a camera and an iPad.

"You guys are nuts," he'd said. "I'm done with that crap."

And Mason was thoroughly enjoying his job. New York City was undergoing a boom in mega-buildings that even exceeded the frenzy of the 1930's, when the 1,250-foot-tall Empire State Building beat out the Chrysler Building and 40 Wall Street for top skyscraper honors. It held its position until 1972, when the 1,368-foot-tall World Trade Center was completed.

It was the collapse of the Trade Center, and New York City's distress over Manhattan's newly ravaged skyline, which many people believe spurred the current construction surge. Since 2001, in addition to the 1,776-foot-tall Freedom Tower that replaced the Twin Towers, a dozen or more skyscrapers, including residential apartment buildings, had been built or were under construction.

Some of the world's most-famous architectural firms were working in Manhattan and its environs. Mason had no dearth of potential stories. Whatever Adler had in mind, Mason thought, it had better be good.

CHAPTER 14 - TRICK QUESTION?

Just after getting back from lunch, Mason got a call from one of Fred Adler's assistants, an Ivy League twerp that Mason thought pretentious.

"Mr. Adler wants to know if you can stop by."

That did not take long, Mason thought. Barry Eliason must have spoken to him right after checking with me.

"Tell Freddie I have to take a leak, and then I'll be over."

Mason didn't have to use the men's room, but he knew the assistant would be annoyed by his nonchalance. He thought the "Freddie" was a nice touch.

After stalling for a few minutes, Mason walked across the room to the area containing the reporters and editors who occupied the Foreign Desk. Adler, a short bullish man with thinning black hair and a small mustache, was on the phone. When he spotted Mason, he held up one finger while he finished his call.

"Tell Soma he's here," Adler said. "Thanks. We'll be right in."

Adler stood and straightened his tie. He was old school, and always wore one.

"Come on, John. She's waiting for us. Good to see you, by the way."

The two men knew each other casually. In fact, Mason liked Adler, who was not as condescending to culture writers as some on the haughty Foreign Desk. Mason knew that was partly the result of some show tickets that Mason had thrown his way. But he suspected that Adler was just a nice guy.

"What's up?"

"I'll let Soma tell you."

This was getting interesting.

***

Mason had met Soma Golde, informally, at various *Times* functions. They knew each other well enough to smile politely in an elevator, but that was all. But he had never been in her office, where he and Adler now sat while she, too, finished up a phone call. Mason was half-convinced that the *Times* had someone whose sole job was to call a bigwig just before a meeting so that he or she could look busy. They were always on the phone it seemed. He looked around. Pictures of her kids on the wall. Various awards amid the books in a floor-to-ceiling bookcase.

Golde, who was speaking standing up behind her desk with her back to them, swirled around as she hung up. She was a very tall woman, with sharp angular features and blond, frizzy hair. As usual, she wore a long, shapeless, dark-colored dress, but it was obvious that there was a lot of attractive woman underneath it.

She sat, and they all exchanged brief pleasantries, and then Golde said, "How would you like to go to Paris?"

They always phrased it that way. Not, "you're going to Paris".

Mason knew it was not really a request. *Times* reporters who wanted to get ahead went where they were sent, no matter how the order was phrased. Mason was not sure he wanted to get ahead, and had been prepared to politely decline any unwelcome

89

offer. He wondered what would have been the reaction if he replied in the negative, if instead of Paris, Soma Golde had said, "How would you like to go to Antarctica?"

But Paris was different.

"Is this a trick question, Soma?"

Both Golde and Adler laughed. But then Golde said something he was not expecting.

"I'm not talking about an assignment, John. It's more like a position."

"I don't understand."

"For some time, I've thought about sending someone to Europe to monitor the dichotomy between the Continent's traditional Western culture, art-wise for want of a better word, and that of the nations represented by the wave of recent immigrants."

"I'm no expert, of course, Soma, but I'm not sure dichotomy is the proper word. It implies mutual exclusivity between disciplines that are opposed or entirely different. Western and eastern art may look different, though not always, but art is art."

Soma Golde took the rebuttal well. Mason had learned that *Times* bigwigs, at least at her level, encouraged debate and individualism.

"I stand corrected. Fred told me you were a pistol."

"I think I said he was a pain in the ass," Adler chimed in.

"In any event, I want someone who can look at all the cultures objectively, and it is obvious that you fit the bill."

"You want me to work in the Paris bureau?"

"No," Adler said. "You won't be assigned to any particular bureau. Stop in to say hello to Julie and her crew. They could prove useful, contact-wise, and maybe you'd want to use one of their desks occasionally."

Juliana Basilone was the Paris bureau chief, and a rising star at the *Times*. Mason had met her once or twice, and they'd hit it off. It probably would be politic to let her know when he was in town. And it wouldn't hurt to make sure they weren't working on the same stories.

"Since we thought you could start with a piece, maybe a series, on the ongoing reconstruction of Notre Dame," Adler continued, "Paris would be a natural place for you to live. But later, if you are more comfortable somewhere else, Rome or London, say, we can have that discussion. We envision you as being a reporter without portfolio, as the diplomats might call it."

All the arguments Mason had prepared about New York being the center of architecture evaporated.

"I can live with Paris, for a start," he said.

Like most people, of any faith, he had been shocked and saddened by the videos of the fire that devastated Notre Dame in Paris. He was sure that he wasn't the only one watching the cathedral's huge spire tumble into the flames who was reminded of the collapse of the Twin Towers at the World Trade Center during the 9/11 terrorist attacks.

Mason paused.

"The Notre Dame thing isn't going to be a religious story, is it? The *Times* probably has better people able to handle that end."

In combat, the "no atheists in foxhole" cliché was very strong. Like many veterans, Mason prayed while under fire. But after two tours and much horror, he was now solidly agnostic. He wasn't about to give up on the idea of God just yet, but organized religion left him cold. And the Catholic Church's sex scandals sealed the deal for him.

Adler smiled.

"I thought you were a Catholic. You keep throwing Villanova and its two national championships in my Big Ten face all the time."

Adler had gone to Purdue.

"Actually, it's three. You forget 1985." Mason smiled. "I didn't say I didn't believe in miracles."

"I haven't the vaguest idea of what you two are talking about," Golde said.

She obviously was not a college basketball fan.

"But you needn't worry, John," Golde continued. "We want your insights into art and architecture on the Continent. I can't promise you that you won't run into some true believers, but most Europeans, particularly the French, are very secular. To them, Notre Dame is a symbol of France, not religion."

"There are true believers and there are true believers," Adler said. "I know this might not be politically correct, but not everyone in France's immigrant community is an art lover. The ISIS nuts even blow up Islamic art."

"That's true," Golde said, smiling. "But this is hardly a combat assignment. I'm sure John has had enough of that."

"How long is the posting?" Mason asked.

"Typically, an overseas assignment is for a

minimum of two years," Golde said. "But this isn't a typical position. We can play it by ear, if that's all right with you. Of course, this is sort of a promotion, so a raise goes with it, as well as some overseas pay."

"Combat pay without the combat, John," Adler said.

"When would I leave?"

"Well, I presume you have some things to clean up here in New York. The *Times* will pay reasonable relocation expenses. Is moving a problem for you?"

"Not really. I have a lease but it's coming up for renewal in two months. I might lose some cash."

"We can probably help you out there, too, if it comes to that. And I don't mean to pry. But you are unmarried, right? No personal entanglements?"

Golde smiled when she asked.

"Nobody will miss me except a few bartenders, Soma."

That wasn't quite true. There were a couple of young women, Mason knew, who might miss his attentions.

"Well, then, I guess you're good to go. How does the first of the month sound?"

As he walked backed to his cubical, Mason reflected that at least he wouldn't have to run in the damn Montauk Mini-Marathon. And French cuisine was certainly a fair trade-off for lobster rolls.

As for women, well, he was going to Paris.

CHAPTER 15 - THE MAHDIS

Nowhere was France's broken immigration system more evident than in Paris, where some neighborhoods were now almost entirely Muslim.

People could trip over women, wearing black burkas head to toe, holding out plates and begging outside tourist sites. Feeling sorry for the poor women, the tourists were easy marks, unless a Parisian told them that the women were probably one of many wives sent out by a single husband to collect money from the unsuspecting. The money was added to the welfare checks the family received.

Abdul Mahdi was no beggar, and despised those who abused the system. They reinforced the Muslim stereotype that right-wing Europeans used to gain political power. He believed that an Islamic takeover of France and the rest of Europe was inevitable, but also believed that the beggars and welfare cheats would only delay it.

Mahdi had a job. A good job. As an Assistant Curator in the Louvre's Department of Near Eastern Antiquities, he was a respected member of the French establishment. Although, as a Muslim immigrant, he despised much of that establishment.

Despite his Islamic leanings, Abdul Mahdi loved the Louvre. When he wasn't working in his own department, he spent hours roaming the museum's six other galleries.

On any given day, he could be found staring up at *The Winged Victory*, the huge sculpture of a draped woman whose lack of both arms and a head does not diminish its thrusting energy. If tourists struck up a conversation with Mahdi, often as not, they would get a lecture about how French archeologists discovered the statue in the Aegean seaport of Samothrace in 1863.

After the Louvre closed, Mahdi often visited his favorite paintings. One of course, was *The Mona Lisa*. During regular museum hours the area around the small painting was always mobbed. Mahdi liked to study *La Jaconde*, as the masterpiece was known to experts, alone.

Not that it was his favorite painting in the Louvre. In fact, when pressed, Mahdi would contend that it was not in his top five. Those honors went to Rembrandt's *Bathsheba at Her Bath*, Delacroix's *Death of Sardanapalus*, Watteau's *Pierrot*, Vermeer's *The Lacemaker*, and Ribera's *The Clubfooted Boy*, although their respective positions in his artistic pantheon frequently changed.

Abdul Mahdi and his older brother, Raisul, had emigrated legally to France a decade earlier from the Sudan. Both had been educated in France, spoke the language fluently and were almost entirely assimilated. Raisul was an engineer, and also had a good job, with Veolia, an energy conglomerate. The brothers were in their 30's and lighter-skinned than many Sudanese. They were often taken for Algerians, which was not an advantage in France.

They were not married and resisted the attempts by some of their friends' mothers to arrange suitable matches. This prompted rumors that they were gay, which was far from the truth. It was just that neither brother was particularly religious, rarely attending a mosque except during a holy day, and then mostly for show. They liked to play the wide-open field that was Paris.

But both were proud of their last name, and told everyone who would listen that they were descendants of Muhammad Ahmad bin Abd Allah, a leader of the Samaniyya order in Sudan who adopted a mystical interpretation of Islam.

Muhammad Ahmad was proclaimed the Mahdi by his disciples, the redeemer of the Islamic faith, and revered for leading a revolt against British rule that led to the death of Major-General Charles George Gordon, who was killed at the Governor-General's palace in Khartoum. Fanatics ignored the Mahdi's orders to spare Gordon, and the famous British officer's head was presented to him. The Mahdi brothers had a print of the famous picture depicting the ghastly ceremony.

They lived in what many consider the Arab quarter of Paris, sharing an apartment in Barbès, in the 18th Arrondissement. Raisul kept in touch with some of the more radical elements in the Arab community, including those who swore allegiance to ISIS.

"For the day, when we come to power," Raisul told his brother as they sat in their small kitchen sharing a bottle of araki, the potent Sudanese liquor made from fermented dates. Araki was illegal in Sharia-observant Sudan, which was another reason they liked living in France.

"For the day," Abdul said, drunkenly.

He also longed for that day, but he was in no hurry. He'd read an article in *Le Monde,* which noted that the European birth rates of the "native" English,

French, German, Italian and other populations were below what some people called "cultural replenishment", while immigrants from the Middle East, Africa and India were producing large families.

Nevertheless, when the fire devastated Notre Dame, Abdul Mahdi had joined thousands of others watching in sadness and disbelief from the banks of the Seine. While European history was not the history of his people, he respected the art it produced.

So, when Marcel Olert, the administrator of his department, called him into an emergency meeting to ask if he would help preserve some of the treasures from Notre Dame he did not hesitate.

"We think the safest place for the art and statues will be in Denon, in the first-floor rooms where we now store the pieces we are still trying to identify from the war," Olert had said. "At least we have some space there. Not like in Sully or Richelieu. I wish I could move the art higher, but you know how tight things are. At least Denon has the most-powerful pumps at the Louvre. We can't have artifacts that survived a fire at Notre Dame ruined by water!"

Abdul Mahdi agreed. The historic Seine floods in January 2018 had threatened masterpieces exhibited on the ground level and below at the Louvre. And Mahdi knew something else: most art works in museums around the world are not exhibited. The floods had also endangered thousands of Louvre treasures held in storage in various departments. The near catastrophe had frightened the authorities into funding a new 100,000-square-foot, hermetically-sealed facility now being constructed near the city of

Liévin in northern France.

"Better safe than sorry, Mahdi," Olert had continued. "We don't want a repeat of the Matsukata incident!"

That was a reference to *Water Lilies: Reflection of Willows*, a 1916 Monet that Japanese collector Kojiro Matsukata bought sometime in the 1920's. It had gone missing until discovered, apparently water-damaged in an earlier flood, by a French researcher in 2016 — in storage at the Louvre!

"That World War II stuff has been there forever," Mahdi said. "I thought someone was going to categorize it."

"You should have seen what we had before you got here," Olert, said, laughing. "Some real dreck. We've been slowly going through it. What's left are mostly the crates the Nazis dumped here. They contain paintings and sculptures those thieves assumed could be used to fill out the galleries they had emptied out."

"The Louvre didn't exhibit them?"

"We might have been defeated, but the curators at that time were not stupid. They would not insult the public with crap."

From what little Western history that he knew, Mahdi believed that the Nazis were just a crazier version of European politics. But he also agreed that they had execrable artistic taste.

"So, most of it stayed crated," Olert continued. "Neither East or West Germany wanted anything back during the Cold War, for ideological reasons. The Germans have loosened up quite a bit since the reunification. The rightists, especially, seem very nostalgic about the Nazi period. There is even a market now for some of Hitler's landscapes, poor as they are. His dream was to be an artist, not a politician. Just think, if he had not failed the entrance exam of the Academy of Fine Arts in Vienna before the first World War, there might not have been a Second."

"Do you think there are some of his paintings in those crates?"

"I doubt it. I can't believe Hitler would send the Louvre anything of his, but who knows? Just look through them. Maybe you can find something interesting."

The chances of that, Mahdi knew, were slim.

"I appreciate you doing this, Abdul. It's not the most edifying job. It will be dusty and dirty. You had better wear some old clothes."

CHAPTER 16 - FATHER VARIALE

Father Alfred Variale was a familiar, and welcome, presence at both Notre Dame Cathedral and the Louvre.

Born in Camucia, Italy, a small town near Cortona in Tuscany, he completed his primary and secondary school education in Florence before earning a Bachelor's Degree in the Department of Humanities at Università degli Studi in Trieste. From there he entered the priesthood and was ordained in the Congregatio a Sancta Cruce (Congregation of Holy Cross), the missionary order founded in 1837 that established high schools and colleges throughout the world, including what became its most-famous educational institute, the University of Notre Dame in South Bend, Indiana.

Although originally established in Le Mans, France, the Holy Cross order is now based in Rome, where Variale spent a year before being sent to the United States to complete his education at Notre Dame. There, he accumulated a Ph.D in Fine Arts and a Masters Degree in Architecture, and became fluent in English. By the time he left South Bend, he was a rabid Notre Dame football and basketball fan, much to the annoyance of his soccer-loving friends back in Italy.

On returning to Rome, Father Variale was posted to the Vatican Museums in Vatican City, home to immense collections of sculpture and paintings, many of them Renaissance masterpieces collected by popes over the centuries. Dating from 1506, the series of galleries in the museums hold some of the world's greatest works, including the Sistine Chapel, the

Raphael Rooms and the Borgia Apartment. He felt he was living in a dream world; not only asked to help in cataloging existing treasures, but also tasked with deciding what stored or newly acquired works would be displayed to millions of visitors.

So, when Notre Dame Cathedral was damaged by the fire, he was the natural choice to be sent to Paris as part of the international effort to save or restore the edifice's artifacts during the cathedral's restoration.

Variale was thrilled to have been sent to Notre Dame, which is both the geographic and historical heart of Paris.

To the uninitiated, the cathedral's enormous stained-glass windows were merely beautiful, as were most such windows in churches and cathedrals the world over. But to a cleric who was also an art historian, Notre Dame's were priceless.

Of course, Variale had visited the cathedral before – one did not work at the Vatican Museums and not travel to see the wonders of Paris – but he came armed with an encyclopedic appreciation of what each window represented. He had even given a series of lectures back in Rome on the great rose window on the cathedral's western façade, which depicts the entire history of the Old Testament's Jewish people from Creation until they reached the "Promised Land" in ancient Israel.

But Variale did not limit his efforts to preserving the stained-glass windows. Also to be protected and preserved were the kneeling statues of medieval French royalty carved by Antione Coysevoix and Guillaume Coustou, and the statues of Christ's ancestors in the Gallery of Kings.

Upon his arrival in Paris right after the blaze, Variale was distraught to find the huge pile of parched timber that had once been the cathedral's attic, and the remains of the famous spire, now filling much of the ground floor before the altar. But he was soon relieved to learn that much of Notre Dame was still structurally sound, and that many of the artifacts had been saved by courageous firemen who, as he reported to his superiors back in Rome, "risked their lives to rescue the soul of France". During the fire and its immediate aftermath, those works had been temporarily moved to City Hall.

Still, there was much work to be done at Notre Dame because the fire had left the interior of the cathedral open to the elements. Vast gaps in the roof had to be covered, tarps stretched over leaks, scaffolding erected to reach certain artifacts and, of course, bracing to protect against further collapses.

Although the portly priest, whose love of French cuisine was only exceeded by his devotion to Italian food, looked nonathletic, his body contained a seemingly endless reservoir of energy. He had played club sports and tennis during his university days in America. Paris is a concentrated city, easily traversed by biking, another of Variale's enthusiasms. When he found the time, he pedaled to the British Embassy, located on Rue du Faubourg Saint-Honoré in the 8th Arrondissement, which has a pristine grass tennis court on its grounds. His friendship with the British Ambassador's counterpart in Vatican City ensured access.

Indeed, Variale made friends wherever he went. And his willingness to get his hands dirty and do some heavy lifting, did not hurt. Moving remaining artwork to the Louvre to join those pieces already saved was paramount, as was the restoration of damaged items. And, of course, all of the collection had to be cataloged.

One of his closest friends at the cathedral was an American, John Mason, a *New York Times* journalist. Not only did they share a love of art, but coming from rival American universities, they could banter and trade friendly barbs over sports that left most of the other workers at Notre Dame cold. Variale and Mason soon became solid drinking buddies. Although wine is king in France, they were able to find a bistro that stocked L'Amalthée, a local brew that satisfied their cravings for beer.

Variale's friends at the Louvre quickly gave him a free run of the museum. The priest, who always seemed to be in a hurry, was even provided with an electronic key pass that gave him access to most of the storerooms in the Louvre. His friends among the workers, police and artisans teased him, saying that the only reason he didn't lose weight during his dozens of daily trips back-and-forth between Notre Dame and the Louvre was the fact that there were so many patisseries along his route. Variale, who never met a croissant he didn't like, jocularly agreed with them.

Variale had met Abdul Mahdi several times, and liked him. He knew that some Parisians, traumatized by terrorist attacks, were suspicious of a Muslim who had such an important position at what many considered the cradle of French art. But Variale knew that Mahdi loved *all* art, as did the many people, of all faiths, from all over the world, who were working as volunteers at the Cathedral.

If anything is truly ecumenical, Mahdi told him, it is art.

CHAPTER 17 - THE CYLINDER

Abdul Mahdi soon realized that Marcel Olert had not been exaggerating when he said sifting through old World War II wooden crates in the crowded storeroom would be a dirty job. Many of them had layers of dust, inside and out. The Administrator's suggestion about wearing old clothes was a good one. At the end of each day, Mahdi and the few workers he'd dragooned into the project looked like street vagabonds.

But at least they could see what they were doing and the working conditions were not unduly onerous. The building they were in, one of the older parts of the Louvre Palace not connected by the central gallery under I.M. Pei's iconic glass pyramid where tourists entered, had been somewhat refurbished. The first-floor storeroom in which they labored was climate-controlled and had new overhead lighting. It even had a door with key-pass entry.

Not that there was anything valuable to protect. As he and Olert expected, most of the "artwork" in the crates was abominable. Germany had historically produced some of the finest art and cultural artifacts in Europe, but none of them were represented in these particular crates. The Nazis taste in art, as in just about everything, was known to be tainted by their rabid anti-Semitism. They glorified traditional "Germanic" paintings and statuary. Mahdi had no great love of the Jews, but he separated art from ideology. Like most experts, he considered most of the German art produced from 1933 to 1945 dull and uninspired.

And not only experts shared that view.

"Man, this is a piece of crap," one of his three-man crew, a simple workman more interested in soccer than art, uttered on seeing the contents of one crate, a statue of some Greek goddess. "Look, one of her tits is chipped off. The plasticine clay my kid uses in school looks better."

Mahdi wholeheartedly agreed, although he did not say so aloud.

Still, he found the categorizing work fairly interesting. Every now and then he came across items that he suspected might fetch something at auction. Those, he removed from their crates and sent to an appropriate department for evaluation. The Louvre could always use a little extra money.

The rest of the materials Mahdi left as he found them, careful to mark each crate with a number that corresponded to a list he made of its contents. The Louvre donated works to other museums all over the world that were not as picky. It was good public relations, and made room for the Paris museum's quality artwork. The other museums could advertise that such-and-such exhibit was "donated by the Louvre". Their ticket sales, and prices, would correspondingly rise.

It was rumored that some of the extra money from those exhibits found its way back to the French museum.

By the second week of the inventory, the men on Mahdi's work crew had reached the far wall of the storeroom.

"Look at the size of that bastard," one of them said, pointing at what was easily the largest crate they had come across.

The crate was crafted of heavy-duty plywood that appeared to be 20 millimeters thick. Mahdi took out a tape measure. The damn thing was 4 meters long, 1.2 meters high and 1.2 meters across front to back. There were six smaller crates stacked on top if it. The entire conglomeration took up a good portion of the rear wall.

"I wonder what the hell is in that thing," another worker said.

"Probably a statue of Kaiser Fucking Wilhelm," the third worker said. "Look, it's almost quitting time. Let's wait until tomorrow to finish."

All three sweating men looked hopefully at Mahdi.

He didn't want to quit so close to the end of the task. He was anxious to get back to his regular duties. But he knew the men were all basically volunteers who were doing him a favor. And, after all, it was Friday.

"I'll tell you what," Mahdi said. "Just get the smaller crates down, and then you can leave. Enjoy your weekend. I'll go through the rest on my own. No use everyone staying."

The men were happy with that.

***

After the workmen left, Mahdi, intrigued, started with the big crate. Because it had others stacked on top, it was cleaner than most of those he'd dealt with. It was sitting atop two wooden pallets, which brought the top to Mahdi's chin level. Thus, opening it was difficult. Mahdi began to regret not at least asking the men for help before he let them go. But using a crowbar, he managed to jimmy open the lid.

Mahdi peered into the crate. He was both astounded and perplexed. It did not contain a statue.

Inside was a long metal cylinder, dull-gray in color, which almost completely filled the crate. Thick metal frames at each end and in the middle, connected four thin tubes, encased the cylinder. Two rectangular metal boxes, one at the middle and the other at one end, sat atop the cylinder. At one end, what appeared to be a larger tube protruded from the cylinder. It had something engraved on it.

Mahdi leaned in to read the engraving. He wiped away a small sheen of rust. He recognized the language as German: *Krupp Konzern (Essen Fabrik)*.

Next, Mahdi examined the boxes. They were locked and also had a bit of rust. But like the rest of the apparatus, whatever it was, the boxes looked almost pristine. You have to hand it to the Germans, he thought, they might have been lousy artists, but they were terrific engineers.

Abdul Mahdi ran his hand along the cylinder. It was warm to the touch!

What could still emanate heat after more than 70 years?

Mahdi had no idea about that, or what the cylinder was meant to do. But, instinctively, he knew that the cylinder was dangerous. It certainly had nothing to do with art.

The Nazis hid it for a reason, and their reasons were usually malevolent.

Mahdi closed the crate's lid and resealed it. He had to use a few new nails from the workbench to augment the crate's original ones, some of which had been bent out of shape when he had pried the lid open.

Abdul Mahdi decided that he was not going to tell Marcel Olert, or anyone else at the Louvre, about his find.

He also decided that he was not anxious to leave the storeroom job after all.

Especially since he knew someone who might be able to tell him all about the strange cylinder.

CHAPTER 18 - THERMAL IMAGES

"It is warm to the touch?"

"Yes," Abdul Mahdi said.

"Was it sitting near some sort of heat source? Those storerooms are heated, are they not?"

"Barely, Raisul. They keep them pretty cool, to protect the artwork."

"I thought you said much of the contents in the crates was shit."

"It is, but the entire floor is climate-controlled. What do you think? They are going to heat just that one room?'

"I'm just speculating."

"For Allah's sake, brother, stop speculating. You are an engineer. What could generate heat after more than seven decades sitting in a storeroom."

Raisul Mahdi ignored his brother's impatience. He was a good engineer. He asked questions.

"The whole cylinder generates heat?"

Abdul Mahdi sighed.

"Yes." Then he thought about it. "Although it does seem hotter at each end. Well, not hotter. I mean warmer."

Raisul face changed. His brother knew the look well.

"You have an idea what it is, don't you?"

"I have an idea what might be generating the heat," Raisul said. "But I must look at it."

"I thought you'd want to."

"Can you get me in?"

"Yes. On the weekend. No one will be working in that part of the building. Perhaps a guard will make the rounds, but they all know me. I can tell them you are my brother and came to help me with my cataloging.

"I am your brother."

"You know what I mean. We can lock the door. No one will bother us."

Raisul Mahdi was lost in thought.

"Doesn't the Louvre have x-ray machines to study art. You know, to authenticate things."

"Yes."

"Can you get your hands on one."

"Certainly. They are portable. I've used the EVO 160D several times on statuary, looking for cracks.

"So, you know how to work it."

"Of course."

"You won't need a technician?"

"It is simple."

"You have trouble with the TV remote, Abdul!"

"That is more complicated, believe me."

Both brothers laughed.

"Will anyone be suspicious?"

"No. In fact, it will appear that I am just being careful with some of the artifacts. But the EVO x-ray has a very small focal point. It can't show us what the insides of the entire cylinder looks like, just small portions."

"That's OK. I'll bring a thermal imager from work."

"How big is that?"

"Hand held."

***

Raisul Mahdi ran his hand along the cylinder, and then touched it at each end, removing his hand

111

quickly.

"See," his brother said.

"Just as I surmised. I think it is radioactive."

"Radioactive!"

Abdul stepped back.

"Probably from decay," Raisul said. "Hand me the red device in my bag."

"Not the imager?"

"No, the other one."

Abdul reached into the large athletic bag they'd brought. It was on a roll table, on which sat the EVO x-ray machine.

"What is it?"

"A Geiger Counter."

It began clacking as soon as Raisul Mahdi brought it near the cylinder. The clacking increased when he brought it to each end. He checked the readings closely.

"I wouldn't want to sleep with this thing," he said. "But short exposures shouldn't hurt us. Your x-ray machine is probably more dangerous. Let's get to work."

***

An hour later, the Mahdi brothers sat on a nearby crate drinking coffee from a thermos. They had taken dozens of x-rays and thermal images of the cylinder.

"The heat sources are concentrated at the ends and have warmed the entire thing," Raisul said.

"What is in the ends?"

"Probably uranium. What you have discovered, little brother, is a bomb."

Abdul Mahdi almost dropped his cup of coffee.

"A bomb!"

"An atom bomb, to be precise. Look at this drawing."

Raisul had sketched as he went along.

"See these conical plates at each end. Those are shaped charges. Probably filled with ordinary explosives."

His finger moved.

"But, right here, and here, in front of each plate is the really hot stuff. U-235 would be my guess. Now there, see the faint weld exactly in the middle of this barrel. Really two barrels welded together. I Googled "Krupp" and "Essen". Krupp was Germany's biggest steelmaker. It turned out weapons for the Nazis. Essen was its headquarters. That's where this contraption was probably fabricated. Whoever built it welded two cannon barrels together. All these wires here, here and here, are designed to fire the charges at each end simultaneously. Each piece of uranium is slightly radioactive but basically inert. But if they are smashed together, they start a chain reaction."

Raisul Mahdi smiled.

"And boom."

"How do you know all this?"

"You are the artist. I'm the engineer. The company I work for, Veolia, has contracts with Électricité de France, which manages most of the country's nuclear reactors. Nuclear power supplies most of France's electricity. I worked on several of them. Fessenheim, Belleville Chinon, Saint- Laurent. That's how I recognized the thermal images."

"But what of the bomb itself? The shaped charges, the barrel, all the rest?"

Raisul laughed

"All that information is available on the Internet."

Abdul Mahdi was startled.

"Raisul! Are you looking at Jihadist sites? Are you insane? The Government will brand us as terrorists!"

"Do not worry, brother. The information about making an atomic bomb is on regular Internet sites. There is more on the Web than the pornography you like so much. Constructing a bomb would be easy. The hard part is getting enough U-235 or plutonium."

Raisul Mahdi pointed at the crate and its cylinder.

"But it would appear that the Nazis managed that."

"How big an explosion are you talking about?"

"I don't know. But probably big enough to level a lot of Paris."

Abdul Mahdi needed a drink. He reached into the canvas bag and brought out a bottle of araki. Both brothers took healthy swigs.

"Raisul, why would the Germans put a bomb here?"

"The Nazis were crazy. Hitler was crazy. He was losing the war. Maybe he wanted to go out with a bang."

"Is it still dangerous? Can it still explode?"

"Probably, with a little tinkering. But I wouldn't worry about it accidentally detonating."

"Why not?"

Rasisul pointed to his crude sketch.

"See these boxes, where the wires come out from? Those are batteries. Pretty corroded after all this time. Dead. And some of the wires are broken. Even if the crate got hit by a bolt of lightning or the place caught fire only the regular explosives might ignite."

"So, it could go off."

"Not the way you think. The blast might kill people standing in this room. But unless both charges went off at the exact same time, to the millisecond, all you'd get is a nuclear meltdown, like Chernobyl. Lots of radioactive waste, which would be unpleasant for the building. Probably couldn't use it for decades. But I don't think that is what the Nazis had in mind."

"I can't just leave it here, Raisul."

"Yes, you can, brother. At least until I talk to someone. You have discovered a gift from Allah."

CHAPTER 19 - CARACAL

The handsome and well-dressed couple that arrived on an Air Canada Boeing 787 Dreamliner from Toronto had little trouble passing through the security checkpoint at Charles de Gaulle Airport.

"How long will you be staying in France?" the Passport Control Officer asked the man.

"At least two weeks, perhaps longer if we decide to visit elsewhere on the Continent," Fabien Caracal replied in the bastard dialect the officer immediately identified as Québécois.

"Business or pleasure?"

"Oh, pleasure," the man said.

The officer stamped the appropriate page on the passport and handed it back. He then picked up the woman's document.

"And you, madame?"

"I go where my husband goes," she laughed.

Her French was marginally better, but still accented. The officer could not place it.

"He's paying for this, after all," she added.

The officer smiled.

"Enjoy your stay," he said, stamping Marie Caracal's passport.

After collecting their luggage, the Caracals took a cab to the Le Meurice. With a two-star Michelin restaurant and Louis XVI furniture, Le Meurice, at 228, Rue De Rivoli, in the 1st Arrondissement, is considered one of the finest hotels in Paris. And at 1,300 Euros a night, one of the city's most expensive.

It was possibly one of the last places anyone would expect one of the world's most-notorious terrorists to be staying.

"Quite a view," Marie Caracal said, standing next to her husband as they gazed at the Louvre from the balcony of their seventh-floor room.

"Let's enjoy it while it lasts," Fabien Caracal replied.

The Caracals were indeed husband and wife. Their names, of course, were false. As were their passports, expertly forged and among the many they used in their assignments on behalf of ISIS.

The Caracal name was also embossed on the JP Morgan Chase Palladium Visa Card they'd used when checking in. It allowed them to avoid annoying charges for foreign exchanges, late payments, cash advances or overdrafts. The card itself did not have a spending limit, and was provided to ISIS, through many cutoffs, by a Saudi prince who liked to stir the pot between the West and the Caliphate.

ISIS did not begrudge the money the Caracals would spend on this assignment, especially since it was basically suicidal. That was fine with both of them. They knew it would probably be their ticket to Paradise. They looked forward to joining their twin sons, killed at two years of age in a French air strike in Syria.

***

Fabian Caracal had been born Jules Caillet to a French father and an Algerian mother in Algiers. After both his parents were killed in a plane crash when he was nine, he was raised by his mother's family in Oran, a coastal metropolis in north-west Algeria.

A wild boy, he was often in trouble and a burden

to his wealthy and conservative grandparents. But he was obviously brilliant, and they secured a place for him at Oran's prestigious German University of Physics. It was there that he was radicalized by disaffected and rabid Islamic students.

It was also there that he met Lotte Wetzel, the woman who now went by the name Marie Caracal. Wetzel was born a Christian in Pulsnitz, a small town near Dresden. She excelled at chemistry and physics at the Ernst-Rietschel comprehensive school and later attended the Hochschule Düsseldorf University of Applied Sciences, which ran an exchange program with Oran. Shortly after meeting Jules Caillet, she converted to Islam, and became as committed to the dream of a Islamic Caliphate as he was.

By 2015, as weapons experts, they were attached to the Al-Khansaa Brigade for the Islamic State of Iraq and the Levant in Iraq. Both distinguished themselves in battle. Lotte Wetzel was known as the Belle of Mosul. In 2017, as ISIS territory collapsed, they decided to flee Mosul with their two children, twin four-year-old boys. Their car, part of a fleeing caravan, was strafed by French warplanes. The twins were killed, and the bereft parents were subsequently captured by Iraqi militiamen.

They were not even allowed to bury their children.

Both parents had been wounded in the air strike, and were taken to a French-run Baghdad hospital for treatment. It was while in hospital custody that Jules Caillet earned his nom de guerre.

Caracals are nocturnal, secretive, felines native to the Middle East and Central Asia. While small, they are known for their savagery. They kill their prey with a bite to the throat. While briefly alone with a single guard, the handcuffed Jules Caillet ripped out the man's throat with his bare teeth. Using the dead guard's keys, he freed himself and then found his wife. Setting a fire on the hospital ground floor and blocking the main exit with their crutches, both of them then disappeared into the night, the screams of trapped patients and staff echoing in their ears.

A month later, they reestablished contact with the remnants of the Caliphate. Without land to defend, ISIS turned to terrorism and murder. Jules Caillet and Lotte Wetzel soon proved valuable, eagerly taking revenge on those they blamed for the death of their sons. They brought several passports — and death — wherever they traveled. The Caracals particularly liked killing Frenchmen.

Even in the brutal world of ISIS, the couple was feared, considered mad dogs. But their unique talents and fanatical loyalty could not be denied. They had assassinated infidels and traitors on three continents. Their successes were such that ISIS looked the other way when the husband-and-wife team indulged their hedonistic and sybaritic tastes.

Marie did not hesitate to use her body. Many targets eagerly took the beautiful woman to bed.

There, she or her husband slit their throats, often during the act of sex.

Still aroused, Lotte sometimes asked her husband to make love to her next to a still-warm corpse.

***

"Decadent," Marie Caracal said, sipping her Martel L'Or.

"But delicious," her husband replied.

They were sitting side-by-side in two of the deep leather armchairs in Bar 228, Le Meurice's opulent lounge famous for its bartenders' ability to produce any of 300 cocktails. They had eaten dinner at the hotel's Restaurant Le Dalí and were now enjoying cognacs and the music of a jazz quartet. Bar 228 was, of course, frequented by hotel guests, but it was also a favorite meeting place among the elite of Parisian society. It was a gilded crowd, and the Caracals fit right in, hiding in plain sight.

"If the Sudanese are right about what they found in the Louvre," Fabian Caracal said, gesturing at the other patrons with his brandy glass, "these fools will soon be ashes."

He started chuckling.

"What is so funny, Jules?"

He looked at her.

"I mean, Fabian."

"Do you know the history of this hotel?"

"No."

There was slight annoyance in her voice. Lotte loved her husband, and thought he was one of the most intelligent men she'd ever known, but like most wives, she found it annoying when he constantly took the opportunity to prove it.

"Le Meurice was the Paris headquarters of the German Army in World War II."

"How interesting."

She stifled a yawn. It had been a long day.

"How ironic, you mean."

"I don't understand."

"The German commander, General Dietrich von Choltitz, lived here during the occupation. Probably sat in this very bar drinking schnapps. Undoubtedly, he had a room with a wonderful view of the Louvre, just like we do."

"I bet he didn't have to pay 1,300 Euros a night, or whatever the going rate was back then."

"Choltitz was a very interesting fellow. He was loyal to the Nazis for most of the war. Even bragged about how many Jews he'd killed. But toward the end of the war, Hitler ordered him to destroy Paris. He refused. That's all anybody remembers. Saved his reputation. Now, we sit here at Le Meuritz planning to do exactly what Choltitz wouldn't. The irony is that had he made an effort to blow up some things, Hitler probably wouldn't have planted his bomb in the Louvre. In saving Paris, the good general sealed its fate, albeit three-quarters of a century later."

He signaled a waiter for two more cognacs.

CHAPTER 20 - CITY OF LIGHT

Although Raisul had assured him that the people
he was meeting were unknown to the police, Abdul
Mahdi was still nervous. He had never before taken
part in any illegality, let alone something that was
assuredly a terrorist act. And he had a healthy respect
for France's intelligence services, which had been on
high alert for many years after a series of bloody
attacks by Islamic fanatics.

That was another thing. Abdul did not consider
himself a fanatic. He had no problem with the
occasional terrorism, especially when it was done in
response to Western military actions against fellow
Muslims. But he believed that Islam would triumph
in Europe in the long run. There was no need to kill
for killing's sake.

The bomb he'd discovered at the Louvre was
another matter entirely. In the hands of the right
people, it could be a deterrent to Western military
power. In the Middle East, it could turn the tide.

"We have to figure out a way to get it moved out
of Paris," he'd told Raisul.

"We don't have the resources to do that," his
brother had insisted. "But some of my friends do."

The Mahdi brothers were sitting on a bench in the
Tuileries Garden between the Louvre and the Place
de la Concorde.

"And they will help us. But they insist on seeing
the bomb first. They are sending two experts to look
at it. Can you get all of us in to see it?"

"That shouldn't be a problem. They already know
you allegedly helped me in the storeroom. I can just

say I found more volunteers. But who are these people? Scientists?"

"Apparently. A husband and wife. Very highly regarded by the Caliphate."

A Frisbee landed at their feet. A young boy ran over.

"Pardon," he said.

The boy picked it up and ran off.

"I never could throw one of those things right," Raisul said.

"When do we meet them?

"Tonight. We are to be on the Ile de la Cité dock for the 6:15 Bateaux-Mouches dinner cruise. They have reserved a table."

"Bateaux-Mouches?"

"What can I say? They are pretending to be tourists."

***

The man who called himself Fabian Caracal slowly ripped into small pieces the sketch that Raisul Mahdi had provided him during dinner. Both the man and his wife had studied it.

"Do you have any other renderings?"

"No. And I am happy you ripped that one up."

"Quite so. What about the thermal images?"

"I did not make copies. But I can describe them."

"Go ahead."

Raisul Mahdi did, in detail, as Caracal listened intently. Both Mahdis got the impression that he did not ever have to write anything down. When Raisul finished, Caracal asked some very specific questions.

"Very good," Caracal said. "You must be an excellent engineer."

"Thank you. What do you think?"

"I think I want to look at it."

Caracal looked at Abdul.

"I understand that you can arrange that."

"Yes."

"We must have total privacy."

"The door to the storeroom will be open until you get there. Once you arrive, I will lock the door."

"What type of lock?"

"Electric key pass."

"Can we get in tomorrow?"

Abdul Mahdi did not like to be rushed.

"I thought early Sunday morning would be better. Most Parisians will still be sleeping. The building where the item is stored will only have a skeleton staff."

"I only want to get a look at it. We did not come to Paris on holiday."

Mahdi shrugged. Perhaps the sooner he was rid of the bomb, the better.

"Then, tomorrow. I will make sure I am working alone."

"What time?"

"Come after lunch. It will be quieter in the building as a whole. I will leave word with the guard. They know Raisul."

Caracal smiled.

"Good. Have some more wine?"

Abdul Mahdi needed more wine. While outwardly civilized and even urbane, Fabian and Marie Caracal exuded an air of menace. During their dinner on the small cruise boat, he had noticed how both of them looked at other passengers. They had cold eyes.

Without knowing exactly why, Abdul feared them.

He screwed up his courage.

"If my find is what my brother thinks it is," he said, "you will get it out of Paris, won't you?'

"I already told you they would," Raisul said.

"That's all right," Fabian Caracal said. "I don't mind answering his question. Yes, of course. We will arrange to remove it."

"You are worried about the Louvre, aren't you, Abdul?"

It was the first time the woman had spoken in quite some time.

"And Paris, Madame."

"Of course. The City of Light."

She put her hand over her husband's and smiled.

"We are thinking about it also."

"Yes, the City of Light," Fabian Caracal said. "The City of Light."

CHAPTER 21 - TRENTE-SIX

Claudette Lebel had nothing but respect for the men and women working in BRI, the "Anti-Gang Brigade" at 36 quai des Orfèvres. She, of course, knew and liked many of them.

But she was a homicide detective, and she also knew she'd been sidelined.

For her own good, of course, but it still annoyed her.

Superintendent Gerard was shrewd, she had to give him that. He had tried to make it seem as if her new "assignment" at Notre Dame was crucial.

"The fire was probably an accident," he had said, "but I would like you to go over everything with your usual diligence, Claudette. Just in case it was arson."

She had argued that she was a murder expert.

"No one died, sir. And shouldn't the sapeurs be in charge of that sort of thing? Their arson investigators are first-rate."

The Brigade des Sapeurs-Pompiers de Paris is the French Army unit that handles fire and rescue in Paris. They had distinguished themselves when the cathedral caught fire. Several of their members were injured saving artifacts.

"I don't think we can rule out terrorism," Gerard said. "The Internet is alive with hints that the fire was set deliberately. Just this morning, Facebook was flooded with conspiracy theories."

Europe was rife with disinformation, spread by individuals and state-run hackers trying to destabilize various electorates and governments. Police departments across the Continent had set up special units to monitor, and counter, the attacks. They were not having much success.

"Most of that is crap, sir. The Russians, left and right-wing bozos, fools looking to make some money from their websites, all sorts of nuts. There were no real indications of terrorism at Notre Dame. And even if there was, that's a job for the DGSI."

The Direction Générale de la Sécurité Intérieure handled internal security in Paris.

"Yes, yes. I know. I don't take it all seriously. But we will look like fools ourselves if we don't check it out. As for DGSI or GIGN, I don't like being cut out of everything. Are their initials better than ours? I won't step on toes until I have to, you know that. But keeping a step ahead of them wouldn't hurt, would it?"

Gerard seemed to be going through a phase when he stuck his nose in everybody's business.

"But why me, sir? You have some junior people who could handle this."

Gerard took out his pipe. He rarely filled it. Mostly, he just gnawed on the well-chewed stem. But Claudette Lebel knew the affectation for what it was. His mind was made up. The interview was effectively over.

"Do I have to order you to do this, Lieutenant? It's only for a month. You can work out of the old Trente-Six. You can walk to Notre Dame from there."

Claudette Lebel had given in. Gerard had been good to her, and not just because she came from a famous French police family. Unlike some bosses she'd dealt with, he truly was not a sexist, and gave female officers in his command a fair shake. She suspected it was because he had three daughters.

Lebel now occupied a desk in a small cubbyhole in the BRI department. She was basically on her own, with no one to answer to. Her "job", as she understood it, was to go over the ground others had, and keep her eyes and ears open.

Never one to let grass grow under her feet, Lebel spent a lot of her time at Notre Dame making sure the cathedral's security was up to snuff. No one, terrorist or careless worker, was going to damage Notre Dame further on her watch.

But she was careful not to get in the way of the serious work that was going on, and she quickly won the respect and affection of the construction workers and art restorers at Notre Dame. Many of the latter came from all over the world and were happy to share their knowledge. Claudette, who never thought of herself as particularly artistic, was soon fascinated to learn things new to her.

One expert, a Catholic priest on loan from the Vatican in Rome, became a close friend. They'd hit it off almost immediately. Claudette's Italian was limited, but Alfred Variale spoke almost perfect English, which was her second language. The balding, roly-poly cleric had inexhaustible energy, and dragged Claudette all over the cathedral. She brought him croissants at all hours, which they shared while drinking his strong black coffee from one of several thermoses he always seemed to have stashed in various alcoves.

And if it was late in the day, Variale would produce a flask of bourbon, which they also shared, sometimes in the coffee, sometimes right out of the flask.

"Jack Daniels," Variale explained once. "Actually, it's sour mash. I acquired a taste for it when I went to school in the States."

Claudette, like most Frenchwomen, was an inveterate wine drinker. But after wincing a few times when drinking the Jack Daniels straight, she also acquired an appreciation.

She and the priest became so close that he was even able to talk her into occasionally going to the daily Mass attended by some of the 150 people working onsite. Because the cathedral's central altar was considered too exposed and potentially dangerous, the Mass was held in the Chapel of the Virgin in a side alcove. But the priests who celebrated the Mass and all the worshipers still wore hard hats.

She now looked at her watch. It was a bit early to make her rounds, but she knew it was never too early to bring some croissants to Father Variale.

On the walk over to the cathedral, she stopped at a small bakery. When she reached Notre Dame, she quickly found Variale, dressed in overalls as usual, in the huge tent set up adjacent to Notre Dame, where displaced stones from the cathedral were sorted. Only Variale's clerical collar differentiated him from the others in the tent. He was deep in conversation with a tall, bareheaded, man who was scribbling in a notebook.

"Ah, Claudette," Variale said on spotting her, "I want you to meet a heathen friend of mine, one of Villanova's great religious failures but one of journalism's chosen ones. He's just over from America."

Claudette could put up with Americans, but she really disliked journalists, who seemed to exist to make life difficult for the police.

"Hi, I'm John Mason," the American said, holding out his hand.

"Lieutenant Claudette Lebel."

She didn't know why she used her rank.

Mason smiled. It was a good smile. He was very handsome, with a face marred only slightly by a small scar, barely noticeable, on his unshaven right cheek.

"Al has told me all about you," Mason said.

"Then I am at a disadvantage, Mr. Mason. Who do you work for?"

"*The New York Times*. The Cultural Desk."

That was not too bad, she thought.

"I'm afraid I don't understand the Villanova comment. Is that a church?"

"Probably, somewhere. But Al was referring to my university. In Pennsylvania."

"The Notre Dame of the east," Variale said. "It apparently did not do John much good. He won't even come to our Mass."

"I still don't understand. The east of what?"

Both men laughed.

"Al graduated from Notre Dame in the States," Mason explained. "Indiana. Villanova is a few miles from Philadelphia. We were just discussing basketball."

He held up his notepad, and she saw the diagram with X's and O's.

"When I walked up, I assumed you were discussing art."

In unison, both men said, "We were," and laughed again.

Men, she thought.

"Well, I'll leave you to it," Claudette said, handing Variale the bag of pastries. "I'll make my rounds. Save me one. And you should be wearing a hard hat, Mr. Mason."

"I thought you told me all Americans had thick skulls, Claudette," Variale teased her.

Coloring, she looked quickly at Mason.

"I said no such thing!"

"We're in a tent, Lieutenant," Mason said, pointing at a nearby pile of rubble. "These stones have already fallen."

"Do you go into the cathedral?"

"Of course."

"With a hard hat?"

"Usually."

"Usually?"

"Sometimes I forget."

"Don't forget again, Mr. Mason. It's the law."

"Yes, ma'am," Mason said, smiling. "I don't want you putting the cuffs on me."

He paused.

"That way."

Claudette had to smile at his insouciance.

"But there is one condition," Mason continued.

"And what is that?"

"That you call me, John."

"Wear your damn hard hat, John."

"OK, Claudette."

As she walked away, she casually glanced back. Mason was staring at her.

Claudette quickly looked away.

He is a cheeky devil, she thought. Good-looking, too.

CHAPTER 22 - CONTRIBUTIONS

"John, you look like you have been hit with the 'thunderbolt'," Variale said.

"What are you talking about?"

"In *The Godfather*, Michael Corleone sees a beautiful young woman while hiding out in Sicily and is immediately entranced. His bodyguards say he has been struck by the 'thunderbolt'. He woos the girl and marries her."

"I saw the movie, Al. She gets blown up, doesn't she?"

"A minor point. It is a great love story."

"What does it have to do with me?"

"I saw how you looked at Claudette."

"Give me a break."

"And how she looked at you."

"She thinks I'm a dumb Yank."

"If you believe that, you are truly thick-headed, my friend."

"I can't believe this. I'm being tutored in romance by a freakin' priest!"

"An Italian priest, my friend. It is in our blood, even if we can't act on it ourselves."

He sighed.

"Some of us, anyway."

Mason and Variale had discussed the Catholic Church's ongoing sex scandals. They were on the same page about the subject, if in different pews.

Mason brought out his notebook.

"Let's stick to basketball, Al. How about lunch?"

Variale checked his watch.

"Sorry, I have to run. I want to go over to the

Louvre. Want to come?"

"No, thanks. I have some interviews I want to finish up. I'll call you later. Maybe we can meet for dinner."

***

"Abdul, how is life treating you?"

Mahdi was startled, and whirled around.

"Oh, it's you, Father."

"Please call me Al. I've told you that before."

"Sorry, I was expecting someone else. My brother and his friends. They are helping me."

Mahdi's English was almost as good as Variale's. They were standing in the storeroom.

"What can I do for you ... Al?"

"Nothing, really. I just stopped by to see how things are going."

Variale's eyes scanned the room and its many crates.

"It's pretty crowded in here."

"Not for too much longer. We will move some of the old stuff out to make more room for Notre Dame artwork."

Variale looked toward the back of the room.

"That one on bottom against the wall is a big bugger. Takes up so much space. Where will it go."

Despite the air-conditioning, Mahdi felt a trickle of sweat run down his spine.

"It is very heavy. And so wide that with all the other crates between it and the door we thought we'd just leave it there and stack some of the smaller crates on top of it," he said calmly. "We will still have plenty of room for some Notre Dame art."

Variale walked over to it.

"What's in it?"

Mahdi swallowed.

"I don't know. Some ugly Nazi stuff, probably. We haven't gotten around to opening it. Or the boxes stacked on top."

"If there is only junk inside, you can always break up the crate and remove it in pieces."

"Yes, yes. Maybe we will do that eventually. I will suggest it. Good idea, Father. I mean, Al."

Variale wondered if he had overstepped the boundary of friendship by telling Mahdi what to do. The poor man was probably sensitive to any suggestion that he was not doing his job properly.

Variale looked at the crate. With all his work at the Vatican museums, if there was such a thing as a Ph.D in crates, he had one. His practiced eye told him that the crate had been opened recently. For one thing, some of the nails in the lid were shiny. And the crates stacked on top of it had obviously been moved as well.

Of course, that did not mean that Mahdi was lying. Perhaps, someone else had worked on the crates. He decided not to say anything. Again, Mahdi might take it the wrong way. Besides, he had a key to the storeroom. He could always come back later, alone. Something about the crate intrigued him.

"Well, Abdul, I'll leave you to it. Who knows? Maybe we won't even need the room here. There was not as much damage at the cathedral as initially thought."

Variale smiled.

"Allah was good to us," he added, ecumenically.

Mahdi laughed, nervously.

135

Variale turned to leave and almost bumped into three people who had just entered. One of them was Raisul Mahdi, who he knew slightly from a previous visit.

"Raisul, how nice to see you. Your brother told me he was expecting you and your friends."

Raisul's eyes widened and he drew a momentary blank, but recovered quickly when he saw the clerical collar.

"Nice to see you, too, Father. Are you leaving?"

"Yes," the priest said.

He extended his hand to both the man and woman who had walked in with Raisul Mahdi.

"Alfred Variale," he said. "I'm glad you are here for Abdul. He is wearing himself out."

"Fabian Caracal," the man said, "and this is my wife, Marie."

The blond-haired man had the dangerous good looks one associates with a Grand Prix race driver. The woman, with dark hair cut short, high cheekbones and wide-set eyes, would have been truly stunning except for those eyes, which were cold, black and lifeless.

Variale bowed slightly and gallantly kissed the woman's hand, which was also cold.

"Father Variale is helping with the restoration of Notre Dame," Abdul Mahdi said.

"That is commendable," she said diffidently as she removed her hand.

"Yes, Father, what you are doing is truly wonderful," Fabian Caracal said. "My wife and I have been discussing how we might also contribute."

"Contributions are always welcome," Variale said,

laughing.

Caracal smiled.

"Oh, we will surely make a contribution, Father. A substantial contribution."

CHAPTER 23 - PRIVACY AND LIES

"I thought you said there would not be anyone else here."

Although Fabian Caracal spoke calmly, the look in his eyes was murderous. Abdul Mahdi was badly frightened.

"It was just a nosy priest," he stammered. "He's not supposed to be here."

Mahdi rushed to lock the door.

"No one will bother us now," he said, nervously.

Marie Caracal walked over to them.

"I do not see any security cameras," she said.

"They only have cameras in the galleries," Mahdi explained. "No one will be able to see us."

Fabian Caracal considered this.

"And we won't be able to monitor the room, either."

"I don't understand," Raisul Mahdi said.

"Never mind, for now," Fabian said. "Let me see the cylinder."

They all walked to the back of the storeroom and the Mahdis spent several minutes removing the smaller crates from atop the one holding the cylinder.

Then, using a pry bar, they opened the large crate.

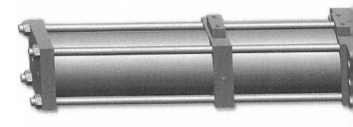

"Fascinating," Fabian Caracal said.

He ran his hand along the cylinder and turned to his wife.

"Warm. Just as they said."

"Will it be dangerous to move?" Raisul asked.

The terrorist glanced at his wife.

"Not after I make some modifications to ensure its safety," he lied. "Now, I need some tools to open the two metal boxes."

"I thought you might," Raisul said. "I left them in that toolbox last time I was here."

He pointed to a workbench off to the side.

"Very good. Now, give Marie and I some room to work."

***

An hour later, Fabian and his wife stood back from the crate.

"What do you think?" she said.

The Mahdi brothers were out of earshot.

"Some of the original wiring has corroded. I wouldn't trust it. But it should be child's play to replace the bad bits and attach some sort of relay that will bypass the timer so that we can detonate the bomb at our leisure. We can get new wiring at a hardware store, and we already have our mobile phones."

Marie was surprised.

"You plan to detonate the bomb remotely? I thought …"

"Don't fret, darling," he interrupted. "We will join our boys in Paradise. Our 'remotely' will be perhaps five feet away. I just don't want to fool with the timer I found. An excellent piece of work, I'm sure. The

Germans were craftsmen. But it's been more than 70 years. I think a little modern technology is in order."

"You don't want to open the cylinder itself?"

"That would be a major undertaking. We might get noticed. And a breach might compromise the barrel's integrity and prevent the proper ignition of the nuclear core. The Germans were also superb engineers. I'm sure they knew what they were doing. Mahdi's sketches and his description of the thermal images are enough."

"But you said the bomb is old. How do you know it will explode?"

"I said the wiring and the timer may have deteriorated. For all practical purposes the uranium lasts forever. As for the traditional explosive charges that will initiate the chain reaction, well, 70 years is no problem. There are bombs lying around Europe from both World Wars that still explode. Again, this is a German bomb. I think we can trust them to build a good one."

Marie Caracal gestured toward the Mahdis.

"What about them? They think we are planning to move the bomb."

"We still need them for a while. After that, we shall see."

He called the other two men over.

"Let's put all this back the way it was," he said, equably. "Here, I'll help you."

"When they finished, Raisul Mahdi said, "Is it as I described?"

"Yes. Praise Allah."

"When will you move it?" Abdul Mahdi asked.

"In a week, perhaps."

"A week!"

"Yes. I have to arrange transport. And won't you need to get approval from the museum?"

"Yes, of course."

"You will have to think up some sort of excuse for moving it."

Abdul Mahdi considered that.

"You are probably right. I can tell my superiors that the crate contains an inferior statue that has been broken. They will just want me to get it out of here."

"There, then it's settled. Now, I must have access to the cylinder all week."

"But why?"

Fabian Caracal adopted a reasonable tone.

"The cylinder looks good. But I am a little worried about the batteries and the wiring. It is corroded. I don't want any accidents during the transport. I want to remove the batteries and some of the wires."

Abdul turned to his brother.

"I thought you said it couldn't detonate accidentally!"

"Your brother was probably right," Caracal said, soothingly. "But trucks crash. They can catch fire. Why should we take a chance? I am a cautious fellow. Speaking of which, I want to be sure no one else knows what we do. I want surveillance in here. Something we alone can monitor remotely."

"But, as I said, there are no security cameras in these storerooms. The administration would never approve that. They are very parsimonious."

"About security?"

"Security in a room full of crap, yes. It would raise questions if I even tried to install something in here.

It's not even my regular department."

Caracal nodded.

"You are right."

He took a moment to think.

"Do you use your laptop in here?"

"Sometimes."

"And no one finds that unusual?"

"Not at all."

"Does it have a camera we can access remotely?"

"I suppose so. If you know what you are doing."

"So, a laptop on, say, that workbench, facing the crate, would not attract notice, would it?'

"No. In fact, I have occasionally left it here overnight by mistake."

"It could be stolen," Marie Caracal said.

"No one would steal a laptop at the Louvre," Abdul Mahdi said, somewhat affronted. "Our security leaving the buildings is excellent."

"I'm sure it is," Fabian Caracal said. "You wouldn't want anyone walking out with the Mona Lisa under their arm, would you? So, it is settled. We will set up your laptop with video feed to mine. I will record everything."

"You can do that?"

Caracal looked at his wife.

"We have picked up a few tricks in our business."

"But who will monitor it?"

Caracal smiled.

"Am I correct in assuming that when the door is closed and the lights are out it is pitch dark in here?"

"Yes."

"So, anyone who comes in here will have to turn on the lights. I don't intend to scroll through hours of video feeds. I can fast-forward to the lighted parts. Hopefully, we will be the only ones who turn on the lights, and I don't think we have to worry about ourselves, do we?"

His tone turned serious.

"Now, Abdul, can you guarantee me privacy during the week? During the day. I don't want to work at night unless absolutely necessary. That might attract too much attention."

Caracal stressed the word "privacy". The implied threat was not lost on Mahdi. He swallowed.

"Yes, of course."

"Good."

Abdul Mahdi seemed to buy all the lies, Caracal thought. He smiled. The batteries and some wiring would be removed. And replaced.

The nuclear bomb would never leave the Louvre. It would never leave Paris.

He would indeed turn France's capital into a "City of Light".

CHAPTER 24 - THE ARK OF THE TOILET

Mason called Father Variale, who suggested dinner at Le Trumilou, a bustling French bistro just across the river from Notre Dame Cathedral. They had dined there before and both were friendly with the owner, a native of Auvergne who knew his cheeses.

When Mason arrived, he was shown to a table in the rear, where Variale was already happily picking at a cheese plate.

Sitting next to him was Claudette Lebel. Both were drinking wine.

"I ran into Claudette," Variale said. "I knew you wouldn't mind if she joined us."

Mason smiled at the "ran into" white lie, which apparently didn't bother the priest's conscience. He was obviously acting as a matchmaker. "Thunderbolt", indeed.

"Of course not," Mason said, sitting down. "I have absolutely nothing against eating with a beautiful woman."

Claudette was surprised, and pleased, at the compliment. For his part, Mason was not merely being gallant. Wherever Lebel was when Variale included her in their dinner plans, she had obviously gone home to change.

It had been Mason's experience that pretty French women looked good in just about anything, but when they make an effort to dress up, they could take your breath away. And Claudette Lebel, in a simple black frock that demurely accented her cleavage and long legs, was a knockout.

The portions were huge at Le Trumilou, and traditionally shared, so they ordered a platter of beef bourguignon and another of steak frites. And, of course, more wine.

Mason and Claudette Lebel were soon engrossed in each other, to the point that they both eventually realized they were virtually ignoring Variale. Not that he minded. His mission was accomplished, and he had more food to himself.

But during one spell where the other two paid him some notice, he said something that peaked Mason's interest.

"And Mahdi was secretive about what was in the big crate?"

"Not exactly secretive," the priest said. "But he did seem to want to change the subject. And I know he had probably opened it. You know Abdul, don't you, John?"

"Sure. Met him a couple of times when I was at the Louvre doing some interviews. Seems like a nice guy. But if he was stonewalling you, that crate must contain something very interesting."

"What do you think it could be?" Claudette asked. "Something valuable? An undiscovered masterpiece? Perhaps, he wants it for himself. Maybe, to sell?"

"Ah, that's the detective in you, my dear," Variale said. "Abdul Mahdi is as honest as the day is long. If there is anything artistically valuable in that crate, which I doubt, he is keeping it secret from the public only. He would tell the Louvre, so it can make a big splash. But this is all conjecture, of course."

Mason insisted on paying for their dinner. He offered to see Claudette home. She was sorely tempted. But she hesitated.

"I'll just take a cab," she finally said, thinking that things were moving just a bit too fast with the handsome American.

Mason walked her to the curb while Variale stopped to chat with a patron he knew.

"Are you free for lunch tomorrow, Claudette?"

There was no hesitation this time.

"Yes."

She handed him her card as she got in a taxi.

"Just call me."

After she was driven off, Mason turned to see Variale come out the door.

"I'd like to get a look at whatever Mahdi found, Al. Want to run over to the Louvre tonight?"

"Ah, always the reporter. I never should have told you that I had a key pass."

"Come on, Al. You are dying to look in that crate, too."

***

Because of their work at Notre Dame, both Variale and Mason were familiar to the security staff at the Louvre. And the priest's key pass gained them access to the ground-floor storeroom where Mahdi worked. It was empty, and very dark. Variale flipped on a light switch.

"It's on the back wall," Variale said.

They walked to the crate.

"We'll have to move those smaller ones," Mason said.

"I shouldn't have had so much wine," Variale said.

"Let's just be careful," Mason laughed. "I don't want to drop a crate that has the Ark of the Covenant

146

in it."

A half hour later, the large crate was uncovered.

"We need some tools," Mason said.

"I'll get that pry bar," Variale said, pointing at a nearby workbench. As he walked away from the bench, he noticed the open laptop. It was not plugged into anything. He assumed the battery was running down, so he shrugged and closed its lid.

They pried open the crate.

"What the hell is that?"

"I have no idea," Variale said. "It looks like some sort of conduit, maybe for a sewer line?"

He peered closer.

"*Krupp Konzern (Essen Fabrik)*. German. That fits. Mahdi said this is all stuff the Germans delivered here while they occupied Paris. Maybe they were trying to fix up the place."

"Great. We just discovered the Nazi plan to redo the Louvre's plumbing! The Ark of the Toilet."

"Well, someone else is interested. Look at the crates on top. They've been moved again, since the last time I was here."

"Are you sure?"

"I know my crates," Variale said.

"I'd love to ask Mahdi about it," Mason said.

"How can we? He'll know we've been snooping."

"Yeah. Well, let's put all this stuff back the way

we found it. Mum's the word."

A guard was making his rounds when they left the storeroom.

"Working late again, Father?"

"Just checking some things, Charles. How is the family?"

"Another one on the way."

"Good work! Europe needs children."

On their way across the interior courtyard of the Louvre, Mason and Variale passed the iconic I.M. Pei pyramid. The priest punched his friend on the arm.

"So, are you going to ask Claudette out?"

Mason laughed.

"You are a troublemaker, Al. But I'm way ahead of you. I'm having lunch with her tomorrow."

"Ah. My work is done, grasshopper."

CHAPTER 25 - PHONE CALLS

Mason called Claudette Lebel the next morning.

"I have some stories to file, so I won't be at Notre Dame. But we can meet for lunch. Do you know where Chez Ajia is? It's not far from the cathedral."

"I know it."

"The food is Asian. Taiwanese, actually. Is that OK?"

"Chez Ajia. Rue du Roi de Sicile. The best Chinese and Thai food in Paris. I know where it is."

She laughed.

"So does every Parisian."

"Oh, crap. I'm sorry. I forgot that you live here. I mean, I know. Oh, the hell with it."

Claudette was still laughing. Soon, Mason was, too. They made a date for 12:30.

***

Abdul and Raisul Mahdi had never been to Le Meurice. The brothers were nervous, having no clue why Fabian Caracal had summoned them. Their anxiety only increased once they entered the Caracal's opulent suite. Fabian was barely civil as he led them over to a laptop computer on a desk. Marie Caracal was lounging on a large white couch. Her eyes never left them as they walked past her. She didn't even nod at their greetings.

The man motioned for them to stand in front of the computer. He tapped a key. The screen was dark. Suddenly it was lighted, and both Mahdis could clearly see the large crate containing the cylinder, with other boxes stacked on it.

"Now comes the good part," Fabian Caracal said.

His voice was like ice.

Two men walked into the frame. Their voices were too muted to understand, but the eyes of both Mahdis widened. Abdul Mahdi turned to Caracal and started to say something.

"Just shut up and watch," the man said.

They watched the two men in the storeroom move the smaller crates. Then, Variale walked over to the workbench and picked up a pry bar. He started walking away but then seemed to notice the laptop. His hand reached up and the screen went dark.

"He closed the laptop's lid," Raisul said. "I wonder if he knew it was recording."

"What difference does that make, you idiot?" Caracal snarled. "They saw what was in the crate. Has Variale contacted you?"

"No."

"Did you recognize the other man?"

The Mahdis looked at each other. Both were badly frightened.

"Well!"

"His name is John Mason," Abdul Mahdi stammered. "He's a friend of the priest."

"What does he do? Does he work at the Louvre? Or Notre Dame?"

"He is a reporter."

Caracal stared at him. His wife came off the couch and whirled Abdul around,

"A reporter! For who?"

Mahdi could barely get the words out.

"The New York Times," he said, swallowing hard.

"The New York fucking Times!" Caracal exclaimed.

***

John Mason was standing in a small group outside the restaurant when Claudette walked up.

"The place is packed," he said. "I guess I should have made a reservation. It will be a while. Do you have a second choice?"

"Do you mean to tell me a big-shot *New York Times* correspondent can't get a table by just snapping his fingers? What happened to the power of the press?"

"The Internet. I can't even get a table at a trendy joint in New York without a reservation."

"Follow me," Claudette said.

When the owner of Chez Ajia saw her, he rushed right over.

"Ah, Lieutenant Lebel. Que c'est agréable de te revoir."

He showed them to an empty table in the rear of the bustling restaurant. On the way, several people at various tables greeted Lebel. As their waiter approached when they sat, Mason turned to Claudette. He mimicked the owner, but in English: "Ah, Lieutenant Lebel. How nice to see you again."

Claudette laughed.

"I am sort of a regular here. I'm sorry."

"Serves me right for telling a Parisian where to eat. And to think I was going to tell you what is good here."

"I always get the chicken with ginger and basil."

Mason laughed.

"So do I."

***

When the Caracals and the Mahdis went to the

Louvre, they fully expected the storeroom and its environs to be filled with police.

It wasn't. In fact, a passing guard greeted Abdul Mahdi cheerfully, as if nothing was amiss.

"It must be a trap," he whispered, nervously.

There was no trap.

They entered the storeroom and turned on the lights. The first thing they noticed was that the large crate was closed and the smaller boxes were restacked on top of it. When they finally opened the big crate and looked at the bomb, Fabian Caracal let out a sigh of relief.

"It doesn't look as if they touched it."

"What do you make of this?" Marie Caracal asked her husband.

"I think we dodged a bullet," he said. "They didn't recognize what the cylinder was. And they put everything back so that no one would know they were here."

He turned to Abdul Mahdi.

"You said that this Mason fellow, the reporter, was interested in the artifacts coming here from the cathedral after the fire."

"Yes. He apparently covers cultural issues for his paper. The priest was probably curious about the contents of the large crate and told Mason, who was probably just looking for a story to write."

Mahdi swallowed hard.

"I don't think any harm was done. But the sooner you move the crate out of here, the better."

"Of course, you are right," Caracal said evenly. "But I don't believe we can take any chances, do you?"

"No. No. What should we do?"

"I want you to call Mason and tell him that you have to see him tonight on an urgent matter. Something to do with Notre Dame. Swear him to secrecy. That will intrigue him."

Marie Caracal looked as if she wanted to say something, but remained silent after a glance from her husband.

"You want him to come back here?" Raisul Mahdi said. "I don't think that is a good idea."

Fabian Caracal stared at him. It was obvious he did not suffer fools gladly. But he remained calm.

"No. Not here. Does he know where you two live?"

"He knows we live in Barbes," Abdul said.

"Does he know the address?"

"No."

"Good. I will give you a Barbes address you can use."

"What are you planning to do with him?"

"That is none of your concern."

He looked at both brothers.

"Is it?"

They shook their heads.

"Now, both of you go stand by the door and make sure we are undisturbed. Marie and I have some work to do. This room is getting more traffic than the Champs-Élysées!"

The Mahdis, chagrined, did what they were told. In fact, they were relieved. Things had worked out better than they expected.

Fabian Caracal began to remove some of the cylinder's old wiring.

"What about the priest?" Marie Caracal asked him.

"Variale is just a dumb cleric interested in paintings. Mason is the dangerous one. He will be dead by tonight."

"But Fabian, we are running out of time. How can we deal with him and finish our work on the bomb?"

"We can't do both. We have people in Barbes who can handle the reporter. I will make a call. And I think it imperative that we finish our work sooner than later. We will have to take a chance and work at night, too."

***

"I'd like to see you again. Can you get tomorrow off?"

"Yes."

For the first time in a long while, Claudette Lebel did not give a fig about work. They had lingered over coffees after lunch at Chez Ajia. She very much wanted to spend time with John Mason.

"I'll take the day off, too," Mason said. "How about we meet for breakfast? Perhaps you can show me some more of your favorite places in Paris."

He smiled. It was a wonderful smile, she decided.

"You seem to know your way around Paris," he teased.

CHAPTER 26 - HUMAN SHIELD

Mason had nothing against taxis, but he had grown to like the Paris Metro. It was fast, reliable and clean, and the stations had easy-to-read maps. And the fact that the maps were in French was not a problem. If anything, they helped him improve his linguistic skills.

Abdul Mahdi's call had been unexpected, but Mason was nevertheless intrigued, as any reporter would be. He readily agreed to keep his visit secret, although he wondered what could be so hush-hush. Had the curator discovered some fabulous piece of art? Or, God forbid, a forgery!

Mason took the Metro to the Barbès–Rochechouart station, where the 9th, 10th, and 18th Arrondissements all converge. He had not yet been in the 18th and was looking forward to checking it off his list. He had five more districts, or arrondissements, left.

Mason had been told that the 18th was one of the city's "most interesting" districts, which was a polite way to say that it was not the safest place for a tourist to visit. Many Parisians looked with suspicion on its varied ethnic enclaves, especially Barbès, its Arabic neighborhood.

"Full of life but sometimes explosive," one guidebook described the 18th. "If you are a little bit adventurous, it's the perfect district for you!"

Mason knew that was brochure-speak for "don't go there". But he was not particularly worried. He was no tourist. In fact, he had served in Arab neighborhoods where the locals shot at him from every door and rooftop. The 18th would be a walk in the park.

In fact, in the early evening dusk he found Barbès utterly charming, full of small shops and a lively open-air market. He passed several restaurants that seemed to cater to every nationality and race and smelled delicious. Although he was pretty sure he couldn't go wrong in any of them, Mason thought he would ask Mahdi for a recommendation.

If he has not eaten, I'll even invite him to dinner, he decided.

Mason probably could have Googled the address Mahdi had given him, 22 Rue Affre, but he wanted to try out his French, so he just asked people for directions. He got himself turned around and stopped outside the Khalid ibn Walid mosque, where a man coming out of a service said he was only a few blocks away.

"That is Rue Myrha over there," the man said, in perfect English. "Make a right and Rue Affre is one more block down."

The man hesitated.

"I would be careful, if I were you."

"Always," Mason said and thanked the man.

When he got to Rue Affre, he understood why the man told him to be cautious. No one was walking about and it was dark. The street was narrow and flanked by old four-story apartment buildings, most looking like they needed work. He thought that perhaps Mahdi should ask the Louvre for a raise.

Mason found the address. There was a black Peugeot parked at the curb in front of the building. He saw the glow of a cigarette from someone sitting

156

behind the wheel. It was not the only car on the street, but for some reason it made him feel uneasy. Perhaps it was the comment the man at the mosque made.

Or perhaps it was the fact that cars with one person sitting in them occasionally blew up in Iraq and Afghanistan.

Mason shrugged. He was being paranoid. What would a suicide bomber be doing on an otherwise quiet Parisian street? No one was going to waste a suicide bomber on a lone pedestrian.

He pressed the buzzer on the door and waited. Nothing happened. He peered through a glass partition. The lobby looked dark. He stepped back and looked up at the windows on various floors. All were dark. One of them seemed to be boarded up.

It was then that he noticed the sign on the wall adjacent to the door. It looked official, with a list of what looked like governmental agencies. But the word that caught his eye, in bold, red letters, was "Condamné".

Mason was confused. Why would Mahdi give him the address of a building that was condemned and obviously vacant? He must have gotten the numbers wrong.

Mason shrugged and began walking back the way he came. He was about 30 feet past the Peugeot when he spotted a man turn the corner in front of him. The man passed under one of the block's few working street lights and Mason could see that he was talking on a cell phone. There was nothing sinister about that.

Until Mason heard a car door close behind him.

He turned.

It was the Peugeot driver, who was walking behind him.

Now, things were sinister.

Mason had always prided himself on his sixth sense, which had come in handy in combat zones. The hairs on the back of his neck actually rose. He was boxed in, caught in the middle.

Of what, he did not know. If he bolted, and the two men meant him no harm, he would feel ridiculous. But ridiculous is better than dead.

Mason could feel the Peugeot man just behind him now. His mind was made up when the man said, "Mason!"

He whirled and ran right at him. The man was taken by surprise and Mason, who saw the gun coming out of the man's pocket, put his shoulder down and rammed into him. Both he and the man went sprawling onto the ground and the gun clattered to the sidewalk.

Mason heard a shout, and then a shot. He felt a burning sensation on the underside of his left forearm. There were more shots, and Mason could see the sparks on the sidewalk where the bullets hit.

He grabbed the man he had knocked over and rolled him on top of himself. He heard three more shots and felt them thud into his human shield, who grunted in pain, then went slack and was silent.

The other man ran up, looking for a clear shot. Desperate, Mason looked around. The gun his dead human shield had dropped was within arm's reach. Mason grabbed it as the surviving gunman fired again, right into his colleague's head, which rocked back and smashed into Mason's forehead.

Mason saw stars and felt himself blacking out, but, firing wildly, he managed to empty the gun he was holding in the direction of the second shooter.

Mason opened his eyes. He must have been briefly unconscious. It was all quiet around him.

He rolled the dead man off and stood up. He could barely see. There was blood in his eyes from a gash on his forehead. When he cleared his vision, he saw the other gunman lying on his back, blood pouring from his shattered throat.

**

The police arrived a lot faster than Mason expected. Two uniformed "flics" pointed their automatics at him until more cops arrived and a sergeant who spoke passable English heard his story and checked his identification.

There was now quite a crowd assembled, and the police cordoned off the scene, blocking the street at both ends. With all the headlights, Mason could see an officer, wearing white gloves, looking into the Peugeot. He said something into his mobile and listened for a minute and nodded. Then he went over to the two bodies and went through their pockets. When he finished that, he walked over to where the sergeant was interrogating Mason.

"La Peugeot a été volée," the officer said. "Ni l'un ni l'autre des raideurs n'avait aucune identification, sergent."

The sergeant nodded and the other officer left.

"The car was stolen," the sergeant said. "And neither man had any I.D."

An ambulance pulled up. Two paramedics got out.

They first went to the two bodies.

"Ne vous embêtez pas avec eux," the sergeant said "Ils vont à la morgue."

They checked the bodies, anyway. Then one of the paramedics came over and began working on Mason's injuries, including a deep rent in his forearm caused by a bullet, and the gash in his forehead.

"This is quite a response," Mason told the sergeant. "Très rapide."

"We get many calls in this neighborhood," the man replied. "Gunshots are not an unusual occurrence. Although this sounded like D-Day. At least that was what the caller said."

"Who called it in?"

The sergeant shrugged.

"I don't understand why I'm not dead," Mason said.

The sergeant understood.

"There were no exit wounds on either body. You were very lucky. They must have been using hollow points."

Mason grimaced at the thought of what a hollow point bullet would have done to the bones of his forearm had it not just been a graze.

"Monsieur, vous avez eu beaucoup de chance," the paramedic said.

"And very good," the sergeant added.

"Officier, cet homme devrait aller à l'hôpital," the paramedic said.

There was blood all over the sidewalk, and plenty of it on Mason. But he knew most of it wasn't his, and that he was not badly hurt.

"I don't need a hospital," he protested.

"I will see you there," the sergeant said, nodding to the paramedic.

The ambulance took Mason to Lariboisière Hospital, nearby in the 10th Arrondissement. The huge hospital, built following a cholera epidemic in 1832, looked old on the outside, but turned out to be modern within. French medicine, Mason had been told, was first-rate, and it was. He doubted he could have had more-efficient care anywhere.

He was swabbed and stitched. His bloodied clothes went into a bag, which he assumed would be turned over to the French police for analysis.

Because he'd had a knock on the head, and, more-likely, because it was a police case with two dead bodies, the doctors who treated him insisted that he stay overnight.

He was given a private room with a police guard. Two homicide detectives, accompanied by the sergeant he'd met at the scene of the attack, came into his room. With the sergeant acting as his interpreter, the homicide cops grilled him until one of his doctors yelled at them to leave.

"Il doit se reposer," the doctor insisted.

As they walked out the door, one of the detectives said "Bruce Willis," and the other one laughed. The sergeant stuck his head back, smiled and gave Mason a thumbs up.

The next thing Mason knew, a pretty nurse came in with a cup of water and a pill. He took both from her.

"A sédatif?"

"Non, pas avec une blessure à la tête," she said, smiling and touching her own forehead. "C'est un antibiotique."

Just as well.

Mason didn't need any help falling asleep.

CHAPTER 27 - A GOOD EXCUSE

Claudette Lebel looked at her watch. Mason was more than a half-hour late. It had been a long time since she'd been stood up. It was only breakfast, but it still rankled her. After all, it had been his suggestion to meet at the café near Cité Universitaire on Boulevard Montparnasse. He had been so damn enthusiastic about it.

Claudette decided to give him the benefit of the doubt. He'd probably overslept. She suddenly realized that she had really been looking forward to spending the day with him.

She ordered another coffee. When that was finished, she called Mason's mobile. Voice mail. She hung up without leaving a message. She didn't want to sound pushy.

"Another coffee, Mademoiselle?"

Claudette looked at the hovering waiter and shook her head.

"L'addition, s'il vous plait."

She sighed and paid her bill. She wasn't going to sit around all morning. The aroma of fresh baguettes and croissants was killing her.

She decided to go to the cathedral.

***

"Did you try his cell?"

Father Variale had not seen Mason.

"Yes."

"He will turn up, I'm sure."

"I want to ask him about architecture," she said lamely.

The priest smiled. He sees right through me,

Claudette thought. I'm acting like a fool in love. Enough of this.

"The hell with it," she said aloud, and headed to Trente-Six. So much for a day off. I should get my head examined. Mason was obviously a typical American. Thoughtless. Arrogant. Self-centered.

She was doing some paperwork when one of the supervisors came over to her.

"I thought you were taking today off, Claudette?"

"My plans fell through."

"Well, then, how would you like an excuse to visit your old pals," the woman said.

"Sure, what's up?"

***

When Lebel got to 36 Rue du Bastion Superintendent Gerard was out, which suited her fine, but two of her old colleagues were there.

"Ah, the sexy Claudette," one of the detectives, whose name was Phillipe Deneuve, said. "What are you doing here? I thought you were still vacationing at Notre Dame."

Both men, whose desks were next to each other, laughed. As did Claudette. They were all good friends who enjoyed teasing each other.

"How is your wife, Phillipe?"

"Ouch. You really know how to hurt a guy."

She sat on the corner of the other cop's desk and high-fived him. His name was Jacques Pepin.

"Seriously," Phillipe said. "What's up."

"Nothing. I just missed you guys. And I was just wondering what you two incompetents are working on."

"I guess it's pretty boring babysitting stained-glass

164

windows," Pepin said.

Claudette Lebel smiled.

"I know that smile," Phillipe said. "Here we go, Jacques. She wants something."

"I heard two guys got shot in Barbès."

"So, you are gone less than a month, on a temporary assignment, no less, and you are poaching for your new bosses."

"They aren't my bosses. But they did ask me to see what you have."

"All we have going is a botched robbery. You could have saved a trip. We were about to send it down to Trente-Six. Two dead, but it looks like self-defense. They tried to rob some American last night, but bit off more than they could chew."

"In the Arab quarter? What was the Ami doing there?"

"Said he was lost."

"Did you believe him?"

"Not sure I did. I suspected he was holding something back when we spoke to him in the hospital. But the self-defense story seems solid."

"He killed them?"

"That's what dead still means, last time I looked."

"Asshole."

"I'm guilty as charged," Phillipe said, laughing.

"What of the American?"

He landed in the hospital, but his wounds are minor," Jacques said. "A real Bruce Willis."

"And he killed them?"

Claudette realized she was repeating herself.

"Deader than bin Laden's dick," Phillipe said. "The Yank grabbed one of their guns. Lucky bastard.

Local cops said it was like D-Day. Lots of shooting. The American apparently used one of the bad guys as a shield. Guy was riddled, but none of the hollows went through him."

"Dum-Dums?" Claudette said, using the police terminology for hollow-point rounds.

"Yeah, they were pros. Bad dudes. No I.D. on them. Stolen car."

"They couldn't have been that good," Jacques pointed out. "They died, not the American. More like Dum-Dum and dumber."

"Fingerprints?"

"But, of course."

He looked at a sheet of paper in front of him.

"Mohamed Mihoubi and Azzedine Fabes. Algerians."

"The gift that keeps on giving," Phillipe said, sourly.

"Both men were on a watch list," Jacques said.

"What kind of watch list?"

"The terrorism kind. Suspected of doing blood work for ISIS sympathizers. The idiots who attacked the American were probably trying to raise funds for whoever hired them. There have been similar attacks on people, tourists, mostly. And some store robberies. Your new pals must be working some of those cases, no?"

"I guess so. I'm not really in the loop down there. They just asked me to check this one out. Anything else I can tell them?"

"We don't have everything back from the lab boys yet, but the guns they used, Kel-Tec 9s, were like the ones from other crimes. Easy to conceal."

"This American. Was he some sort of diplomat? Or a drug dealer? I mean, to ace two pros like that."

"Nah. Guy seemed very legit. He was some kind of war hero, a veteran. No shortage of them around. The Americans have been fighting people for decades. Anyway, he got the better of them."

"He's a reporter, or something," Phillipe said.

Both men noticed the change that came over Lebel.

"A reporter?"

"Yeah," Jacques said. "What's the matter?"

"Mason. John Mason."

The men looked at each other.

"That's him," Jacques said.

"Oh, my God!"

"Don't tell me he is a friend of yours. I thought you hated reporters."

"And Americans," Phillipe chimed in. "And men in general."

Claudette ignored the jibes.

"I met him at Notre Dame. He is doing a story on the restoration. I was supposed to meet him for breakfast. I thought he stood me up."

"What man in his right mind would stand you up, sexy," Phillipe said. "Without a good excuse, I mean."

"Which this guy had," Jacques said.

"Almost the best," Philippe added. "Dead would have been better."

"What hospital is he in?"

"Lariboisière," Jacques said, "but he may have been discharged by now."

"I'll check. Do you have his home address?"

167

She tried to sound nonchalant. But her partners saw through her.

"The lovely Claudette is contemplating a house call, Phillipe. I think she might be smitten."

"It certainly sounds like it."

Lebel gave them a friendly finger as she left.

But it didn't stop her from wondering if they weren't right.

CHAPTER 28 - UNPROFESSIONAL LOVE

Claudette Lebel called Lariboisière Hospital, and was told that Mason was still there.

Except by the time she got there, he wasn't.

"You just missed him, Lieutenant," the duty physician told her. "He is a tough bird. We wanted to keep him for observation for another day, but he checked himself out. He took a bad knock on his head and some stitches where the bullet grazed his arm, but otherwise he was in fine fettle. He said it wasn't his first rodeo, whatever that means. But he promised to rest at home today."

Lebel thanked him and was about to leave.

"But he also said he had to stop at his office first."

Claudette called Variale.

"Does John have an office in Paris?"

"Not really. Why?"

She told him.

"He probably meant the *Times* Paris Bureau. I know he stopped by there occasionally. What was he doing in the hospital?"

"I'll tell you later. Thanks."

Next, she Googled the *Times* Bureau. It was located in the Bourse, in the financial district.

"You just missed him," a receptionist told her. "He said he had to get something from the safe. Then he was heading home, I think. He was in a car accident."

So, that's what Mason is telling people.

She called his mobile. Voice mail.

Claudette berated herself.

I'm acting like an idiot, chasing Mason all over Paris.

But she headed toward his apartment.

***

Mason lived in a small third-floor flat near the Place de la Bastille in the 11th Arrondissement. It is a quiet neighborhood with many gardens, and is popular with unmarried Parisians of both sexes.

When Mason opened the door, Claudette could see that he was holding a small automatic in his left hand.

"Claudette," he said, and put the gun on a table next to the entrance.

"May I come in?"

"Yes, of course."

Mason stepped aside. He was barefoot, and was wearing slacks and a t-shirt. There was a bandage on the underside of his left forearm. His hair was wet.

"I just got out of the shower," he said.

"I called you 20 minutes ago."

"I take long showers."

"Did you get the gun from the safe at the *Times* Bureau?"

"Yes. How did you know?"

"I just came from there."

"Why were you there?"

"The doctor at Lariboisière said you were going to your office, and Father Variale suggested that was what you meant."

Mason smiled.

"You've spent a lot of time and effort in finding me, Claudette."

"Do you have a permit for that gun?"

Claudette had no idea why she asked that.

Mason smiled.

"Are you here to arrest me?"

"Of course, not. I just came to see how you are. When you did not show up for breakfast, I was concerned. No one could reach you. So, I went to work. And it was still only happenstance that I found out what happened."

"I'm sorry. I know you tried to reach me a few times. I saw your number on my cell phone. I should have called you back."

"You are damn right about that!"

Her anger was palpable. Mason grinned.

"Want some wine? Or something stronger?"

Her anger dissipated.

"Stronger."

"Scotch?"

Claudette nodded and Mason went to the kitchen to fix their drinks. She took the opportunity to look around the apartment. Simply furnished, it was much neater than she expected. Mason probably had someone in to keep it up. She glanced through a door and saw his bed. At his approach she quickly looked away. They sat on opposite ends of a couch in his living room.

"Does your arm hurt?"

"Fortunately, it's not my drinking arm," he said, and took a healthy swallow. "Are you still angry with me?"

"A little. But why didn't you call me?"

"I guess I was working out what I could tell you. I don't think I want to lie to you."

"What were you doing on that street, in that neighborhood, at that time of night."

"I told the police I was lost, and it was my own fault I got mugged."

"You lied to them?"

He looked bemused.

"John, why the gun?"

"Paris is proving to be a dangerous city. Maybe I'm scared."

"You just killed two very tough men. You are a war hero. I'd say you don't scare easily."

"Why, Claudette, you've been checking up on me. I'm flattered. But for the record, I only killed one of those men. The other was killed conveniently acting as my shield. Not by choice, I admit."

"What's going on?'

"Do you want to know as a cop, or as something else."

"As a police officer, of course."

Mason smiled.

"Now who is being untruthful?"

He put down his drink and stood abruptly. So did she.

"This interview is over," he said.

Claudette was shocked. But before she could reply, Mason pulled her close and kissed her, hard, on the mouth.

She broke the kiss, and sputtered.

"What do you think you are doing?"

He looked at her. They were silent for a moment.

"Oh, Jesus," she said.

Her hand went around his neck and this time she pulled his head down for a kiss. Now, there was no hesitation. They did not even break the kiss as Mason's arm slid down and he picked her up and headed to the bedroom.

***

Claudette was sitting naked at the edge of the bed. Mason reached over and stroked her back.

"I don't know why I did that," she said, primarily to herself.

"I don't know why either," Mason said. "Do they teach that particular maneuver to all French girls in school?"

Claudette turned to look at him. Her face colored.

"I didn't mean that, you idiot. I meant I don't know why I wound up in your bed. It is so unprofessional."

"I'll let the 'unprofessional' remark go," he laughed. "But I will remind you why we're in bed together."

His hand moved around her torso and gently grabbed a breast. She moaned and slid down into his arms.

***

An hour later, they lay, exhausted, in each other's arms.

"I think this may be more than just un quickie," Mason said.

Claudette tweaked him where men don't like to be tweaked.

"Ce n'était pas si rapide,"

Mason laughed.

Claudette stroked his face.

"Quoi maintenant, ma chérie?"

"Now, I'll tell you why I was on that damn street."

***

"You should have told the detectives that the man knew your name! Phillipe and Jacques are my friends."

"I did not know that. And even if I did, I might not have told them."

Lebel started to protest. Mason put his finger on her mouth.

"Look, Claudette. I am a reporter first, and a victim second. The attack was obviously planned. Mahdi set me up. I want to know why before the cops muck things up."

He saw the fire in her eyes. She was truly beautiful. He kissed her again.

"Sorry. I didn't mean it that way. But I smell a story. A big story. And it has something to do with that crate. And what's in it. I'm pretty damn sure this is not about Nazi plumbing."

"They may kill you the next time."

"Life is a crap shoot. I'll be lucky to get out of this bed alive."

She ran her fingers over some small scars on his chest. There was another small wound on his shoulder that had not been there an hour earlier. Claudette colored, and suppressed a smile.

"I am an officer of the law!"

"Then arrest me. Although, as I've said before, I was hoping that you would have other uses for your handcuffs."

"Tu es un bâtard!"

"My mother would disagree. Will you help me? I need some time."

She looked deep into his eyes.

"I shouldn't."

A pause.

"But I will."

Claudette stayed the night at Mason's flat. They

made love again in the morning. Then she said she had to go home and change.

"I'll also stop by Rue du Bastion. I want to make some calls."

They agreed to meet at Notre Dame at 11 AM.

CHAPTER 29 - SUSPICION

"What happened to you?" Father Variale said, when he saw the bandage on Mason's forehead.

"It's a long story. Let's go get some coffee."

The three of them walked to a nearby boulangerie. On the way, Variale noticed that both Mason and Lebel scanned the area, and took a table at the back facing the front.

He noticed something else. From the way they sat and talked, it was obvious that they were a couple now. Probably lovers.

"Ah, France," he said.

"What was that?" Mason asked.

"Nothing. So, what happened?"

Mason told him.

When he finished, Variale said, "You must have written down the wrong address, John. Have you called Abdul?"

"No. I wanted to talk to you first, Al. I don't make that kind of an error. I even read it back to him when he called me."

"I checked the address this morning with the Office du Logement," Claudette said. "The building at 22 Rue Affre has been unoccupied for almost a year. And I went further. Abdul Mahdi doesn't even live on Rue Affre. He lives at 68 Rue Nicolet. And has for years."

"No one gets the number *and* the street wrong," Mason said. "By accident."

"What are you saying?"

"Mahdi set me up. I was ambushed."

"But why?"

"You told me he was honest. But how well do you really know him?"

"I've seen him often enough when I stop by the Louvre. I considered him a friend."

"Hold that thought, Al," Mason said. "I'll get us some more coffee."

"One of those raisin croissants couldn't hurt," the priest said.

While Mason went to the counter, Variale turned to Claudette Lebel.

"I'm happy for you two," he said.

"Is it that obvious," she said.

"I'm Italian," he said. "I can spot a love affair a kilometer away."

"Wasn't it dangerous for you and John to go to the Louvre at night?"

"I've done it before. Everybody there knows me. I did feel like we were skulking around behind Abdul's back. But I was relieved that the crate didn't contain anything valuable."

"What did it contain?"

"Just a big hunk of metal. And it wasn't from the Bronze Age!"

Mason returned, with coffee and croissants.

"Diamonds," he said.

They both looked at him.

"Or something just as valuable. Other types of jewels. I suppose gold, too, although I would think they would be too heavy. But gold fillings, rings and the like are possible."

"What are you talking about?" Claudette asked.

Variale slammed his hand down on the table.

"Of course! We did not look inside the cylinder."

"A lot of the stuff the Nazis stole has never been located," Mason said. "They confiscated valuables from the Jews. Even pulled their teeth in the camps, the bastards. If that cylinder is full of gold and diamonds, I don't think Mahdi would turn it over to the Louvre. Nobody is that honest."

"He would have had to look inside," Variale said.

"The boxes on top had been opened, remember? Mahdi opens the crate and sees what to all intents and purposes looks like a huge sewer pipe. He is curious. He opens one of the boxes on top and peers inside. It's full of diamonds, or gold, whatever. Worth millions. Hell, maybe billions now. What is he going to do? He can't just leave all that loot there. But he also doesn't have to get the whole cylinder out, just what's inside. He can do that in increments, but he needs time. So, he tells everyone it's just easier to leave the crate where it is. He even stacks other crates on top, to make sure no one discovers what he has."

"That would still make him a thief. I guess I was wrong about him."

"Maybe he doesn't think he really is a thief. I mean, if I'm right, he might not really be bothered by valuables stolen from dead Jews. Did you ever talk politics with him?"

"One does not talk politics with a Muslim in France," Variale replied. "But Abdul never came across to me as a fanatic of any sort. I know he loved the Louvre. Why on earth would he try to have you murdered?"

"My guess is that somehow he found out that I was interested. That guard we spoke to when we left might have mentioned we were there. We put everything back, but Mahdi probably would have noticed that we moved stuff around."

"But he probably also knew we didn't look inside. We didn't touch the boxes. That would be evident. And I still can't believe Abdul is a killer."

"He might not be," Claudette interjected. "But the people he told about the cylinder are killers."

"What people?"

"The men who attacked John were professionals who worked for ISIS. What's inside that cylinder could fund terrorism for decades."

"Are you now saying that Abdul Mahdi is a terrorist? Just because he is Sudanese? Isn't that blatant profiling?"

"I don't know. Maybe he just asked the wrong people for help. What I do know is that he called John and two trained assassins with terrorist ties were lying in wait for him."

"Why hasn't anyone tried to kill me?"

"Don't take this the wrong way," Mason said. "These people are probably not worried about you. But the last thing they want is some nosy journalist from *The New York Times* writing a humorous story about a crate full of Nazi junk in the Louvre. That might open up a can of worms. And the cylinder."

Variale finished his croissant and began working on another. Neither of his companions had touched theirs.

"What happens if we are wrong? And it is a sewer pipe. I'm having a hard time wrapping my head around the idea that Abdul is a terrorist. He seems so nice. Although ..."

"Although, what?" Claudette prompted.

Variale looked thoughtful.

"When Abdul lied to me about the crate, I bumped into some people who said they came to help him. One was his brother, Raisul. I knew him. But the others were new to me. A well-dressed, chic, couple. Looked like they belonged on the Riviera. The woman was very beautiful, but she had cold eyes."

"Cold eyes?"

"I don't know how else to describe them. Maybe, like shark eyes. And the man, I don't know, seemed a bit pretentious. Now, I wonder. They seemed out of place. And I noticed when I left that Abdul shut the door behind me. He locked it. It could only be opened with a key card."

"Was that unusual."

"Well, yes. During the day the storeroom is open. But they did not look like terrorists."

"Terrorists come in all forms these days," Mason said. "And they might not have been terrorists, but experts in valuables. Perhaps buyers. It all fits."

"We have to be sure," Claudette said.

"Which is why we have to go back and crack open that cylinder."

"When?"

"Tonight. After the Louvre closes. You still have your key card, don't you, Al?"

"Yes."

"And the storeroom will be deserted?"

"It should be."

"Good. The tools already there should suffice. All we have to do is pry open one of those boxes on the cylinder. If I'm right, once we get a peek inside, we can call out the gendarmes."

180

He smiled at Claudette.

"I mean some other gendarmes."

CHAPTER 30 - SURPRISE

Lebel requisitioned a police car from "Trente-six" and met Mason and Variale outside the Denon wing of the Louvre Palace at 8 PM.

Mason noticed the slight bulge under Claudette's jacket.

"You are armed."

"I am a police officer," she said. "What about you? Did you bring your illegal gun?"

"It's against the flat of my back."

"What is this, Iwo Jima?" said Variale. "All I'm armed with is my faith."

"Do you want us to put the guns back in the car?" Mason asked.

"Hell, no," Variale said.

"Praise the Lord and pass the ammunition, Father?"

"Something like that."

"Don't worry," Claudette said. "With any luck, we will have the storeroom to ourselves. Let's go."

When they reached the storeroom, Mason stepped aside to let Variale use his key pass. The door clicked open. They were all surprised to find the room already illuminated. They could see two figures with their backs to them hunched over the large crate against the far wall.

As they walked down the aisle between stacked crates, Variale said, "My God!". He pointed at something sticking out between two crates. A pair of feet.

It was Abdul Maidi. His eyes were open but he was very dead. His brother, Raisul, was also lying between the crates, but further in. Both had neat bullet holes in their foreheads.

Lebel and Mason started to draw their weapons.

"Don't move!"

It was a man's voice. They froze. Fabian Caracal was standing in the aisle, with a silenced automatic pointed at them. Lebel and Mason looked at each other. Two against one.

"I wouldn't if I were you."

This time it was a woman's voice. Marie Caracal came up behind them. If anything, her gun, also silenced, looked larger.

"I'm sorry," Variale said. "They must have heard me."

"Yes, thank you for that," Fabian Caracal said. "We were so engrossed in our work we ignored our normal security precautions. But we are somewhat rushed for time. Now, place your weapons on the floor and put your hands up. Lotte, check them for more weapons."

She did, efficiently.

With a wave of his own gun, Caracal herded his captives toward the big crate.

"Sit on that crate over there," he ordered.

He looked at Mason and shook his head.

"I am surprised we were disturbed, but especially by you, Mr. Mason. Are you not supposed to be dead?"

"The best laid plans," Mason replied.

"What happened to the two men who were sent to kill you?"

"They are as dead as the Mahdis."

"Why did you kill Abdul and his brother?" Variale

183

asked. "I thought you were all working together?"

"We were. And the Caliphate owes them much. I am sure they will be rewarded in Paradise. But when I told them I had no intention of moving the bomb, and was going to set it off here, they became a problem."

"Bomb!" Claudette exclaimed.

"Yes. Abdul Mahdi was worried about the Louvre's precious collection. His brother, well, I think he was worried about his own hide. In any event, they objected and Marie was forced to shoot them."

"What bomb?" Mason asked.

Caracal looked amused.

"Just what did you think was in the crate?"

"Diamonds, jewels, gold. We thought you were trying to smuggle the stuff out."

Caracal actually laughed.

"Wonderful! You took us for common criminals."

"Not common, but the terrorist type."

"Well, you at least got that part right."

Caracal looked at Lebel.

"I know these two, but who are you?"

"Lieutenant Claudette Lebel, of the Paris Gendarmerie. And before this goes any further, I will ask you to surrender before our backup gets here."

It was a bluff, and Fabian Caracal knew it.

"You are both beautiful and brave, Lieutenant. But there is no backup coming, or you wouldn't have come here with these two amateurs."

"I resent that," Mason said. "Maybe you should have a word with the two stiffs I left on Rue Affre."

Caracal bowed his head slightly.

"My apologies. And to you as well, Father. I guess you all deserve credit for figuring out about the cylinder, even if you are wrong about what is in it."

"Listen, Caracal. Why do you need us? Let us go. You can set off your bomb. I'm a reporter for *The New York Times*. Don't you want me to report your manifesto, or whatever you call it?"

Caracal just shook his head.

"Then, at least let Claudette and the priest go. You tried to kill me once. Now, here's your chance to do it right."

"I'm not leaving you!" Claudette said.

"I'm not going anywhere, either," Variale added.

"This is pointless, Jules, let me shoot them and be done with it."

"No, Lotte. They got this far. I think we owe them the full story."

His wife rolled her eyes. Another damn history lesson. As usual, Jules couldn't resist, especially with a captive audience.

"You see, my friends, even if I let you go, there is no place in Paris you can reach that will be safe when our atomic bomb explodes, in the name of ISIS!"

"You must be joking, Caracal," Mason said. "Where the hell would you get a working atomic bomb. And how would you get it in here? ISIS is clever, but not that clever."

"But it is not the Caliphate's bomb. The late Abdul Mahdi discovered it among all the crates the Germans left here in 1945."

"Now, I'm sure you're joking," Mason said. "The Germans did not have nuclear weapons."

"I guess someone will have to rewrite the history

books, my friend. I mean, after we rewrite history in a few minutes."

"I don't believe you."

"If it is any consolation, I was skeptical myself until I examined the cylinder. Apparently, the Nazis were able to craft a working atomic weapon toward the end of the war. It had all the proper parts for a first-generation atomic bomb, much like you Americans dropped on Hiroshima. The Germans added some interesting refinements to the firing mechanism, including, of course, a booby trap. Which I have disarmed. I did not want the bomb activated until I knew everything electrical still worked. Blowing myself up prematurely would not have served the Caliphate's purposes. So, I attached new batteries, some new wiring and such. Much more to my liking. A piece of cake, as you Americans would say."

Caracal held up a cell phone.

"All that I have to do is dial a number and another mobile phone attached to the bomb will ring. When the answering service kicks in, the bomb circuits will close and, well, you know the rest."

"How many rings?"

Caracal grinned.

"A journalist to the end. Three. That was the minimum allowed by the service. I saw no point in dragging things out. And with the amount of uranium they packed at both ends of the bomb, I suspect much of Paris will be leveled. As for why the Nazis put it here, I can only guess that Hitler was planning some sort of revenge. He was insane toward the end."

"There is a lot of that going around," Mason said. Caracal laughed.

"I like you Mason. I read the *Times*. Except for its lies about Islam, it is a good paper. It's a pity you have to die along with us."

CHAPTER 31 - LAST RITES

"So, you are suicide bombers. But why? Surely you could detonate the bomb remotely,"

Mason was stalling for time. Just why, he did not know. The situation was hopeless.

"My wife and I plan to join our children in Paradise. Children the French killed in the Caliphate. Our babies."

Really hopeless, Mason realized. There really was nothing else to say.

"Please, Jules, let's get this over with," Lotte Wetzel said.

She was clearly exasperated.

"Sorry, my dear. Just one more second."

Caracal walked over to Variale.

"Here, priest, this is for you."

He handed Variale a yellow, weathered envelope with "A.H." embossed on the outside.

"What is this?"

"A gift from the Führer, from the grave. Go ahead, open it."

Variale did. He recognized it immediately as coming from a Bible. But the archaic German script meant nothing to him.

"It was in the bomb," Caracal explained. "Lotte was able to read it. Some religious gibberish about cinnamon, angels, prophets and Babylon."

Variale looked up from the fragment.

"Rejoice over her, thou heaven," he recited from memory, "and ye holy apostles and prophets; for God hath avenged you on her. And a mighty angel took up a stone like a great millstone, and cast it into the sea, saying, Thus with violence shall that great city Babylon be thrown down, and shall be found no more at all."

"So, you know it, priest."

"It is from the Old Testament. The Book of Revelations. *Alas, Babylon* is one of the most beautiful passages in Scripture. It foretells the destruction of sinful Babylon."

"Jewish drivel, but appropriate. Hitler must have had a sense of humor. Anyway, keep it. Maybe it will get you into Paradise. You will excuse me. I have to make a call."

He walked away, laughing, and took a cell phone from his pocket. As he started punching in numbers, his wife stood beside him. They held hands and looked upward, toward the heavens.

Claudette Lebel rushed them.

She did not make it. Lotte Wetzel sensed her approach and drew a silenced pistol. She shot Claudette in the chest. Claudette fell backwards from the impact of the round. Mason and Variale rushed to her side. There was a hole on the left side of her blouse, at her heart. But no blood stain. As Mason cradled her in his arms, she shook her head and opened her eyes. He unbuttoned her blouse and saw the Kevlar vest.

"Let me finish them," Lotte Wetzel hissed.

"No," Jules Caillet said. "Let them go. Where can they run?"

The cell phone attached to the bomb's wiring began to ring.

Once, twice, three times. And then the answering service picked up the call.

The Caracals shouted "Allah Akbar!" in unison.

Variale made the sign of the cross, blessing his friends. Mason instinctively covered Claudette's eyes, knowing it was a ridiculous thing to do when they were about to be blown to smithereens along with half the city.

"We won't feel a thing," Mason said.

"My poor Paris," Claudette said, sobbing.

"Our Father, who art in heaven," said the priest.

There was a loud bang from inside the crate. But that was all.

Caracal and his wife turned to see what was happening. A strange, pulsing blue light began emanating from the cylinder. The side of the crate ignited and fell away and though the light was almost blinding Mason could see that the cylinder was melting. In fact, it looked molten!

Marie Caracal screamed. Her hair seemed to catch fire. Mason grabbed Claudette and Variale and pushed them toward the door. They ran as the entire room was bathed in blinding light.

"Don't look back," Mason shouted.

He could feel heat on his back.

They ran through the door, which Mason slammed behind them. The screams coming from inside the room were blood-curdling.

Then, silence.

They started to run down the hallway but Claudette collapsed on the floor. Variale began tending to her. He ripped off her blouse and the bullet-proof vest she was wearing. The bullet had penetrated the vest, but had not gone all the way into her left breast. A trickle of blood ran down from the protruding round. Variale pressed down on the wound.

"You may have to confess this, Father," Claudette said through clenched teeth.

"There goes another vow," he replied.

Mason bent down over them.

"I'm all right," Claudette said. "What happened in there?"

"I don't know, but I'm going to find out."

Mason headed back to the door. He could see museum staff and guards running down the hall toward them. He assumed emergency personnel, firemen and police would be right behind.

"Don't open the door!" Claudette cried.

Mason did not have to. As he approached the storeroom the door opened and two blackened figures staggered out. They were naked and horribly burned. From the way they lurched, Mason realized they were nearly blind.

One of the guards approached them.

"Get back!" Mason yelled. "They are probably radioactive."

The guard hesitated, until Claudette, still lying on the floor, also yelled, "Contaminé. Radioactif!"

The guard froze in place as the two terrorists crumpled to the floor, moaning and writhing in pain as large portions of their skin sloughed off. Mason heard one of the staffers retching. There was nothing anyone could do but watch the Caracals die horribly from radiation poisoning a thousand times the lethal dose.

Their agony was soon over and they finally lay still, wisps of smoke rising from their charred remains.

Mason suppressed his own rising gorge. He chanced a glance into the room. There was a small fire where the crate had been, and what appeared to be a glowing residue of molten metal.

With Variale holding her, Claudette Lebel was now on her feet.

"Tell them to clear the building," Mason said. "All the floors. I think the nuclear core of the cylinder will melt through to the basement and maybe beyond. And let's get the hell out of here."

In a few clipped French phrases, Claudette told the staff and guards to run.

Which they did.

"What about them?" Variale said, gesturing at the bodies.

"They are dead."

Variale started walking to the bodies.

"Al, what are you doing?"

"Everyone deserves last rites," the priest said. "Don't worry, I won't get too close."

Mason was about to protest, but Claudette grabbed his arm.

"It is what makes us different from them," she said quietly, as Variale made the sign of the cross over the Caracals.

CHAPTER 32 - LEGEND

As might be expected in a country that gets 75% of its electrical power from 58 nuclear power plants, not to mention to being a frequent target of terrorists, France has an excellent emergency response system dedicated to dealing with nuclear catastrophes.

Within moments of local authorities determining what had transpired in the Louvre, the entire museum was evacuated and cordoned off, as were two streets in each direction. The Seine was blocked for a half mile up and down river. The airports were closed and overflights of Paris were banned until the authorities were assured that there was no radiation leak into the atmosphere.

There was, of course, plenty of initial grumbling among both citizens and tourists until police trucks with broadcasting systems announced the nuclear danger in several languages. Then, the grumbling ceased and people did the sensible thing and left the area.

Mason, Variale and Lebel were hustled off in Hazmat suits to an isolation unit in a nearby hospital set up for just such an occasion. There they were unceremoniously stripped and given showers. Claudette got special treatment because of her wound, which, while physically minor, presented its own radiation hazard because of the metal bullet that broke her skin. Fortunately, it turned out not to be irradiated.

In fact, none of the three had been near enough to the cylinder meltdown to be seriously affected, although the doctors chided Variale for getting so close to the roasted terrorists when he gave them last rites.

"They said that in addition to everything else, I was endangering my ability to have children," he told Mason and Lebel. "I told them not to worry."

The dead terrorists were another matter. Their corpses were so "hot" that the experts from the military and Electricité de France decided that a proper burial, even cremation, was too dangerous. The bodies were covered in lead blankets and then fork-lifted by a volunteer in a Hazmat suit and deposited in a special truck.

They would be interred later in a lead-lined coffin in a special pit in Civeaux designated for nuclear waste. Some scientists speculated that since even bacteria might not survive in their irradiated corpses, there would not be any decomposition for thousands, perhaps millions, of years. Others argued that bacterial life "would find a way". In any event, it was unlikely anyone would ever know.

Fortunately, unlike Chernobyl, Fukushima and Three Mile Island, there was no real fire, explosion or release of radioactive plumes outside the Louvre storeroom. The core of the Rache Bombe did turn molten and sink through the first-floor storeroom to the basement below, but it missed water pipes and stopped there. The wall behind the cylinder's crate were irradiated and damaged, as were nearby crates and their artifacts.

Thanks to Abdul Mahdi's meticulous inventory, found in his office, it was determined that nothing in the damaged crates was worth saving. Their contents followed Jules Caillet and Lotte Wetzel into the pit at

Civeaux. One French expert sniffed that even a few million years wouldn't increase the value of the Nazi works.

Because of the lessons learned from previous nuclear disasters, the time needed for radiation cleanup was drastically shortened. But estimates of the period needed to eliminate all traces of radioactivity at the museum still ran from one month to one year. But all in all, the Louvre, and Paris, were incredibly fortunate.

As for Mason, Lebel and Variale, after brief stints in the hospital, they were all reunited at the Élysée Palace, where each was awarded The Légion d'Honneur by the President of the Republic. That ceremony was followed by a whirlwind week of interviews and dinners.

"You know, we really don't deserve all this," Mason said at one point while they waited to be introduced at some function.

"What do you mean?" Claudette said.

"We didn't know it was an atom bomb. We thought the cylinder was full of treasure."

"We all tried to set the record straight," Variale said.

"And were told to shut up about it," Claudette said. "In no uncertain terms."

"Print the legend," Mason murmured.

"What did you say?" she asked.

"It's a line in a classic John Ford Western, *The Man Who Shot Liberty Valance*. 'When the truth becomes legend, print the legend'."

"The world needs heroes, John." Claudette said. "Do you want to give up your *Pulitzer*?"

"I haven't won a *Pulitzer*."

"After this, you will."

Mason smiled. She was right. He would probably win a *Pulitzer,* if not for a news story, for the book that New York publishers were already bidding over.

Some people wanted to canonize Variale. And Claudette had been promoted to Superintendent. They had all been contacted about a potential movie. By Steven Spielberg, no less. Correcting the story that had now gone around the world would be embarrassing and disastrous.

Still, Neither Mason or Lebel enjoyed the limelight. Not so, Father Alfred Variale.

"We are the toast of Paris," he commented at one point, his mouth full of foie gras, "because everyone believes we prevented Paris from being toasted."

That was logical. The cylinder had been completely destroyed in the meltdown, so no one knew exactly why there was no nuclear blast. It was assumed that the suspicions of Mason and the others had forced Jules Caillet to rush his preparations, and he had botched the job.

CHAPTER 33 - MADAME FILION

John Mason was sitting alone outside a bistro near Notre Dame having his lunch. It was a month after the incident at the museum, and he was back at work in Paris after a brief trip to the States for more honors, including a ceremony at the White House, and a round of publishing houses with his agent.

He had called Claudette, only to find that she was at her family's vacation cottage in Provence, having finally agreed to take a holiday.

"The house is used mostly in August, when we French typically take our vacations, but it is vacant now. I wanted some solitude. And peace and quiet."

"Well, no one deserves it more."

He tried, but was unable to hide the disappointment in his voice.

Claudette laughed.

"I find that solitude is overrated. And I can do with a little less peace and quiet. I'm here for another week. Can you come? I miss you terribly."

***

"Monsieur Mason?"

John Mason looked up from the book he was reading.

"Yes."

The gray flecks in her short hair gave her away, buy she was thin and attractive, in that way French women entering middle-age can be when they take the time.

"I am so sorry to bother you while you are eating, but Father Variale at the cathedral told me that you might be here."

Her English was excellent, with that lilting French accent that he always felt charming.

Mason smiled noncommittally. He didn't bother asking the woman how she knew it was him. His face had been splashed all over the media in the wake of the Louvre incident. A photo of him carrying the wounded police lieutenant, Claudette Lebel, had gone viral on the Internet. He was, in fact, a national hero, as were Claudette and Variale, the priest now known to grateful Parisians as "le père héroïque".

Mason had even been asked for his autograph. The notoriety was something that he worried might compromise his position at the *Times*, although no one in New York had said anything to him. His editors at the *Times* had been delighted with his decision to stay on staff.

"Yes, Madame?"

"My name is Catherine Filion. I have come to ask a favor of you."

Mason remembered his manners. If Variale told her where he probably was, she was not an autograph hound.

"Please sit," Mason said, and got up to hold her chair. "A glass of wine, or a coffee, perhaps?"

"Oh, no thank you. You are so kind. But I really came at the request of my grand-mère. She would like to see you."

"I don't understand."

"She has just turned 100. She has all her faculties, but she never leaves her apartment now. She read about you in the newspaper."

Mason sipped his wine. He wondered how he could phrase his refusal to visit the woman's grandmother without sounding like a complete boor. He also wondered if he should. Variale would probably give him grief if he blew a centenarian off.

Catherine Filion's next statement solved the problem

"My grand-mère said that she knows why the Nazi bomb in the Louvre did not explode the way it should have."

***

"Thank you for coming, Mr. Mason. My name is Natalie Filion."

Mason grasped the old women's bony hand gently, but her grip was firmer than he expected. Her English was almost as good as her granddaughter's. He and Catherine Filion had taken a taxi to an apartment in the 7th Arrondissement, a wealthy district that was home to foreign embassies and had many international residents.

"Please sit. Catherine, would you be so kind and make us coffee."

Mason sat in one of the two chairs across from her. There was a coffee table between them. Although he knew her age, Mason was a little surprised at how vital Natalie Filion looked and how strong her voice was. He would have said that she didn't look a day over 90, but knew how ridiculous that would sound. He knew people who were 70 who didn't look as good as this woman.

There was a cane leaning against the small table next to her chair. On the table were thick-lensed glasses with mother-of-pearl frames and a large, ornate card. She noticed him looking at the card, and picked it up and handed it to him.

The card was from the "President of the Republic of France" congratulating Natalie Filion on her 100th birthday, and commending her for her World War II service in the Resistance.

"The card came with a proclamation," the old woman said. "Catherine is having it framed."

Mason handed the card back.

"It is an honor to meet you, Madame Filion."

Catherine Filion brought in coffee in a French press and served them. As she did, Mason took the time to look around the third-floor apartment. It was simply, but elegantly, decorated. There seemed to be as many plaques and awards on the walls as there were paintings. Bright light streamed in from doors leading to a small terrace. He could see the Eiffel Tower, only a few blocks away.

There was a tray of small pastries, and Catherine put two on a plate for her grandmother. She looked at Mason, who shook his head. Once they were all settled, Mason said, "Madame Filion, you have something you wish to tell me?"

The old lady smiled.

"I believe I may have saved your life at the Louvre. And, of course, saved my beloved Paris."

CHAPTER 34 - SOCKS

"I was a seamstress in Blois, a city in the Loire valley, near the famous Chambord chateau. Many people don't realize, but the valley had many smaller castles, which have no names but are very grand. To supplement my income, I worked a few days a week at one of them in Cherveny. It was owned by a veteran of the First War, an aristocrat and a colonel of the old school named Sauney. A wonderful man, a nice man, even if he was a Conservative. Me, I am a Socialist, and will be to the day I die. We both hated the Boche, as he called them. Sauney let us use his chateau to hide Allied pilots, until they could be safely moved out of France."

"Then, you were a member of the Resistance?"

"Oh yes. But not for long. The Gestapo rounded up a bunch of us. But for something else, not related to the chateau. Sauney survived the war but had to sell his chateau to make ends meet. Some rich American bought it and restored it, moat and all. I went back for a visit, perhaps 20 years ago. It looked pretty much the same as I remembered. There was even a picture of Sauney in his uniform over one of the fireplaces. And there was a big cloth ledger displayed that had the signatures of the British and American airmen who hid there. The book was in the secret room in the basement and was brought out after the Nazis surrendered."

"That is fascinating," Mason said politely.

"After I was captured, they tortured me for information they already knew, the fools. I mean, they arrested me, didn't they? I think they just did it for practice for when they caught a big fish. I was a minnow. But it wasn't too bad. When they found out I was a seamstress, they sent me to Ravensbrück."

"A concentration camp."

"Yes, exclusively for women. It was located in northern Germany. Mostly Polish and Russians, but thousands of French and Dutch, many of whom were political prisoners, some quite famous. I met the sister of Fiorello LaGuardia, the famous New York mayor. She married a Hungarian Jew and was arrested in Budapest in 1944. But everyone was basically a slave worker. Because I was a seamstress, I was assigned to a textile factory. We made socks for German soldiers. The Nazis kept the factories barely heated in the winter. Sometimes you could see your breath."

Natalie Filion smiled at the memory.

"But we had our revenge. Winter works both ways. We tinkered with the fabric machines and looms so that the socks were so thin they would fall apart when the Nazi soldiers marched. We were responsible for a lot of frostbite on the Eastern Front!"

Mason also smiled, again politely, wondering where the old lady's story was going, and what it had to do with what had happened in the Louvre. Well, he had plenty of time to listen to a story from a hundred-year-old women who presumably did not have much time left at all.

"The Nazis worked us like dogs. Even factory workers had to do heavy labor outside after their shift. Toward the end, we worked seven days a week. No days off. That's how we knew Germany was losing the war. But at least we were alive, fed a few hundred calories more than other inmates, who died like flies."

She took a sip of her coffee.

"Then, one day, the factory wardress, Maria Oberheuser, came in. All of us were told to line up outside. Oberheuser was a beast. 'The Beast of Ravensbrück' is what we called her. A real sadist. She fancied herself as an expert on classical music. She had it playing on loudspeakers throughout the camp. We had to march in step to it. They even played it on the way to the gas chambers. For all I know, they played it in the gas chambers."

She shrugged.

"But who would ever know that? The music blared inside our factory. There was no way to get away from it. We were listening to it when we lined up outside that day. Oberheuser wasn't alone. Dr. Mandel was standing there, with some guards."

Mason looked at Catherine Filion.

"Dr. Mandel?"

"Herta Mandel," the old woman continued, "the camp physician. She used to experiment on the healthiest women in Ravensbrück. Inject rotten wood, tainted blood, rusted shell fragments, even animal feces under the skin and then let it fester, sometimes to gangrene. Then she would try various treatments, including amputations. She said she was trying to mimic the war wounds of German soldiers so the Wehrmacht could better treat them. Many inmates died, so I don't know what was accomplished."

"Good God," Mason said.

"There were other experiments. She injected the youngest women, who were still capable of childbirth, with chemicals to make them stop having their periods. One of the guards told me that the Germans wanted to see if they could stop certain races from reproducing."

Now, Mason wouldn't have stopped listening to the old women's wartime reminisces for the world.

"Oberheuser walked up and down our ranks, and tapped some of us on the head with her riding crop, or whatever it was. Those selected had to step forward. I was one. We were terrified. We'd heard that was how she did it when choosing women for the experiments."

Natalie Filion held out her cup.

"Catherine, perhaps some more coffee. And this time put in some of that brandy the doctor says I shouldn't have."

She looked at Mason.

"I wouldn't mind the brandy without the coffee," he said.

When they were settled again, Madame Filion continued.

Oberheuser had chosen 15 of us. Mandel walked up and down our line. She poked and prodded us, looked in our mouths, like we were horses or something. She told five women to go back into the barracks. They did, glancing at us out of pity. I'm sure they thought the rest of us were going to Mandel's laboratory, or worse. But we weren't."

"Where did you go?" Mason said.

"They took us for showers. Believe me, that scared us even more, because we'd heard stories about the 'showers', which turned out to be gas chambers! But these were real showers, with water. Then we were given clean clothes, and fed. Not a lot, because our stomachs couldn't take it. A little meat and bread. And some sort of green beans. I had not seen a green vegetable for so long, I cried. And I wasn't the only one. Then, we were put on an army truck. As a soldier closed the canvas in the back, he looked in and said, "lucky bitches". And we were. We were driven out of Ravensbrück."

"Where did you go?"

"Orhdruf. In Thuringia. Another concentration camp. A real hellhole. But there was also a factory there. But not for socks. There were many male slave laborers working in it, but the Nazis wanted women who could work with their hands on assembling delicate devices used in weapons. Rockets and detonators for bombs and artillery shells. Women who worked on sewing machines and looms were obvious choices. At least to the Nazis."

Mason was beginning to understand.

"You sabotaged some of the weapons."

Madame Filion smiled.

"It was even easier than the socks. All we had to do was mix in some impurities in the explosive. We were reluctant to work with it, but the technicians told us that it was insensitive to shock. We could drop it and it would not explode. It could even be molded into various shapes. Of course, when we shaped it, we made sure we added a little something when we could. The rooms we worked in were pretty clean, but when no one was looking, we could spit in the charges, or blow our noses and add what came out."

"Oh, grand-mère!" her granddaughter exclaimed.

"Am I being too crude, Mr. Mason?"

"No, ma'am, you are doing fine."

"Then I guess I can tell you that one of the ladies even managed to urinate in one batch."

"Grand-mère!"

Mason laughed.

"Sorry," he said.

"That's all right," the old woman said. "I read about what happened in the Louvre. The description of the bomb you saw sounded a lot like one I caught a glimpse of in the factory. The room it was in was off limits to us, but the door was open when I walked past. I had wondered what it was. It didn't look like any bomb or rocket I'd seen."

Natalie Filion put a bony hand on Mason's arm.

"But I know that some of the detonators we sabotaged that day went into that room."

CHAPTER 35 - PROVENCE

"I was glad I went to see Madame Filion, even though at first I was going to give Al Variale hell for setting me up."

"How is 'le père héroïquet'? He said my breasts reminded him of the Venus de Milo."

Mason laughed.

"And you still have both your arms. Al is fine. He just got back from Rome. He was honored at the Vatican. I think they made him a Monsignor. He sends his love. Where you are concerned, sometimes I think Al regrets being a priest."

"He just likes my croissants."

"Is that what he calls them?"

"You idiot."

John Mason and Claudette Lebel were reclined in lounges beside a small pool next to her family's cottage. He had arrived but an hour earlier. It was his first visit to Provence, a region in southeastern France known for its vineyards and olive groves.

Claudette's cottage was set back from the road adjacent to a forest of pine trees. The only sounds came from the rustle of leaves and birdsong. Below the pool, a rabbit munched in a field of lavender, frequently looking up, alert to any movement and sound. Rabbits everywhere are nervous creatures, possibly more so in France, where they are favorite table fare.

The water in the pool looked inviting, even with the many leaves and petals floating in it. It was early October, but still warm outside.

Claudette also looked inviting. She was wearing a

white bikini, or at least the bottom half. The cottage was secluded, not that it would make a difference to a French woman to be seen topless. Mason had enjoyed Claudette's breasts, but he was nowhere near the point where he could be blasé about them. Variale was right about the Venus de Milo. But Mason tried to ignore them as he recounted everything that Natalie Filion had told him.

"It was fascinating to talk with her. She told me she even saw Eisenhower and Patton when they toured Ohrdruf. She said Patton threw up when he saw the bodies in the crematoria."

"I presume you will write about all of this," Claudette said. "Too few of the current generation know just what went on. Europe never learns."

"I have a piece scheduled for the Sunday Magazine. It's a miracle Madame Filion is still alive to talk about it. In fact, it's a miracle she survived the war at all. She said that the factory was bombed and many of the scientists and engineers were killed, along with many of the slave laborers. But she was lucky."

"Lucky?"

"I guess that is a poor choice of words given her circumstances. But the women from Ravensbrück were housed in a separate building that was not hit. That's where she was when the American Army liberated the camp. She thinks the SS guards forgot about them in their panic to get away. She also said not all of the guards made it. The ones that didn't were beaten to death by surviving inmates, or shot by outraged GI's."

"There are some murders that aren't murders,"

Claudette said. "I hope those horrible women who ran Ravensbrück also paid the price."

Mason became grim.

"I did some research. Maria Oberheuser, the sadistic wardress with a fondness for classical music and gassing women was turned over to the Poles. Apparently 'The Beast of Ravensbrück' killed more of them than any other group. She was hanged in Cracow in 1946. Dr. Herta Mandel was tried by the Americans and sentenced to five years."

"Five years! For her experiments on helpless women!"

"She claimed she was only trying to help the war effort. You know, just following orders. And that's not the worst of it. After she got out, the West Germans restored her medical license. She became a respected pediatrician in Stuttgart. Died of natural causes in 1997."

"Chienne! Chatte! Putain!"

"I love it when you talk dirty. Especially in French."

"Pardon, moi. Do you want me to repeat the words in English?"

"No, I got the drift. Mandel was all of those things, and more."

"Do you think that Natalie Filion's crottes de nez saved Paris?"

"Crottes de nez? That one is new to me."

Claudette smiled.

"I think your American term is 'boogers'."

Mason laughed.

"I don't think anyone will ever know. Someone in that factory sabotaged the detonators, and it was probably her. But I will leave out the scatological stuff in the article."

"No snot or urine?"

"No."

"How boring. I thought the *Times* was 'the paper of record'."

"It's my story. I'll tell it my way. I'm covering up enough already. The Internet would run wild with that kind of thing. Natalie Filion and the other heroes at Orhdruf deserve better. But I threw the unwashed mob a bone. I said spit might have been involved."

"Can you use the word "flegme"?

"Does it mean what I think it does?"

"Yes. Although I think you American barbarians spell it differently."

"Barbarian? I'm a national icon."

Claudette stuck her tongue out at Mason.

"When will the story run?"

"Sometime next month. The *Times* wants to fact-check it to death. Find more Orhdruf and Ravensbrück survivors, if there are any. But it is a solid piece, as is. Natalie Filion will have some more plaques to put up on her wall, if she can find room for them."

"A remarkable woman," Claudette said.

Mason looked into Claudette Lebel's eyes.

"One of two remarkable women I've met in France."

She smiled at the compliment. There was a small puckered scar just above her left nipple, which Mason couldn't help but notice had become erect. As did its mate.

"Does it hurt, Claudette?"

His throat was a little dry.

"Does what hurt?"

"Where you were shot."

She touched the scar.

"Not really. Just a twinge every now and then. Thank God for the vest. The surgeons told me it will be barely noticeable in time, especially if I tanned."

She smiled, and parted her lips.

"Of course, perhaps if you kissed it…"

ADDENDUM A: ALAS, BABYLON
BOOK OF REVELATION 18:10
OLD TESTAMENT, KING JAMES VERSION

And after these things I saw another angel come down from heaven, having great power; and the earth was lightened with his glory.

And he cried mightily with a strong voice, saying, Babylon the great is fallen, is fallen, and is become the habitation of devils, and the hold of every foul spirit, and a cage of every unclean and hateful bird.

For all nations have drunk of the wine of the wrath of her fornication, and the kings of the earth have committed fornication with her, and the merchants of the earth are waxed rich through the abundance of her delicacies.

And I heard another voice from heaven, saying, Come out of her, my people, that ye be not partakers of her sins, and that ye receive not of her plagues.

For her sins have reached unto heaven, and God hath remembered her iniquities.

Reward her even as she rewarded you, and double unto her double according to her works: in the cup which she hath filled fill to her double.

How much she hath glorified herself, and lived deliciously, so much torment and sorrow give her: for she saith in her heart, I sit a queen, and am no widow, and shall see no sorrow.

Therefore shall her plagues come in one day, death, and mourning, and famine; and she shall be utterly burned with fire: for strong is the Lord God who judgeth her.

And the kings of the earth, who have committed

*fornication and lived deliciously with her, shall
bewail her, and lament for her, when they shall see
the smoke of her burning,*

*Standing afar off for the fear of her torment,
saying, Alas, alas, that great city Babylon, that
mighty city! for in one hour is thy judgment come.*

*And the merchants of the earth shall weep and
mourn over her; for no man buyeth their
merchandise any more:*

*The merchandise of gold, and silver, and precious
stones, and of pearls, and fine linen, and purple, and
silk, and scarlet, and all thyine wood, and all manner
vessels of ivory, and all manner vessels of most
precious wood, and of brass, and iron, and marble,*

*And cinnamon, and odours, and ointments, and
frankincense, and wine, and oil, and fine flour, and
wheat, and beasts, and sheep, and horses, and
chariots, and slaves, and souls of men.*

*And the fruits that thy soul lusted after are
departed from thee, and all things which were dainty
and goodly are departed from thee, and thou shalt
find them no more at all.*

*The merchants of these things, which were made
rich by her, shall stand afar off for the fear of her
torment, weeping and wailing,*

*And saying, Alas, alas, that great city, that was
clothed in fine linen, and purple, and scarlet, and
decked with gold, and precious stones, and pearls!*

*For in one hour so great riches is come to nought.
And every shipmaster, and all the company in ships,
and sailors, and as many as trade by sea, stood afar
off,*

And cried when they saw the smoke of her

burning, saying, What city is like unto this great city!

And they cast dust on their heads, and cried, weeping and wailing, saying, Alas, alas, that great city, wherein were made rich all that had ships in the sea by reason of her costliness! for in one hour is she made desolate.

Rejoice over her, thou heaven, and ye holy apostles and prophets; for God hath avenged you on her.

And a mighty angel took up a stone like a great millstone, and cast it into the sea, saying, Thus with violence shall that great city Babylon be thrown down, and shall be found no more at all.

And the voice of harpers, and musicians, and of pipers, and trumpeters, shall be heard no more at all in thee; and no craftsman, of whatsoever craft he be, shall be found any more in thee; and the sound of a millstone shall be heard no more at all in thee;

And the light of a candle shall shine no more at all in thee; and the voice of the bridegroom and of the bride shall be heard no more at all in thee: for thy merchants were the great men of the earth; for by thy sorceries were all nations deceived.

And in her was found the blood of prophets, and of saints, and of all that were slain upon the earth.

ADDENDUM B: ADOLF HITLER'S LAST WILL AND TESTAMENT

More than thirty years have now passed since I in 1914 made my modest contribution as a volunteer in the first world war that was forced upon the Reich.

In these three decades I have been actuated solely by love and loyalty to my people in all my thoughts, acts, and life. They gave me the strength to make the most difficult decisions which have ever confronted mortal man. I have spent my time, my working strength, and my health in these three decades.

It is untrue that I or anyone else in Germany wanted the war in 1939. It was desired and instigated exclusively by those international statesmen who were either of Jewish descent or worked for Jewish interests. I have made too many offers for the control and limitation of armaments, which posterity will not for all time be able to disregard for the responsibility for the outbreak of this war to be laid on me. I have further never wished that after the first fatal world war a second against England, or even against America, should break out. Centuries will pass away, but out of the ruins of our towns and monuments the hatred against those finally responsible whom we have to thank for everything, international Jewry and its helpers, will grow.

Three days before the outbreak of the German-Polish war I again proposed to the British ambassador in Berlin a solution to the German-Polish problem—

similar to that in the case of the Saar district, under international control. This offer also cannot be denied. It was only rejected because the leading circles in English politics wanted the war, partly on account of the business hoped for and partly under influence of propaganda organized by international Jewry.

I have also made it quite plain that, if the nations of Europe are again to be regarded as mere shares to be bought and sold by these international conspirators in money and finance, then that race, Jewry, which is the real criminal of this murderous struggle, will be saddled with the responsibility. I further left no one in doubt that this time not only would millions of children of Europe's Aryan peoples die of hunger, not only would millions of grown men suffer death, and not only hundreds of thousands of women and children be burnt and bombed to death in the towns, without the real criminal having to atone for this guilt, even if by more humane means.

After six years of war, which in spite of all setbacks will go down one day in history as the most glorious and valiant demonstration of a nation's life purpose, I cannot forsake the city which is the capital of this Reich. As the forces are too small to make any further stand against the enemy attack at this place, and our resistance is gradually being weakened by men who are as deluded as they are lacking in initiative, I should like, by remaining in this town, to share my fate with those, the millions of others, who have also taken upon themselves to do so. Moreover I do not wish to fall into the hands of an enemy who requires a new spectacle organized by the Jews for the amusement of their hysterical masses.

I have decided therefore to remain in Berlin and there of my own free will to choose death at the moment when I believe the position of the Fuehrer and Chancellor itself can no longer be held.

I die with a happy heart, aware of the immeasurable deeds and achievements of our soldiers at the front, our women at home, the achievements of our farmers and workers and the work, unique in history, of our youth who bear my name.

That from the bottom of my heart I express my thanks to you all, is just as self-evident as my wish that you should, because of that, on no account give up the struggle but rather continue it against the enemies of the Fatherland, no matter where, true to the creed of a great Clausewitz. From the sacrifice of our soldiers and from my own unity with them unto death, will in any case spring up in the history of Germany, the seed of a radiant renaissance of the National-Socialist movement and thus of the realization of a true community of nations.

Many of the most courageous men and women have decided to unite their lives with mine until the very last. I have begged and finally ordered them not to do this, but to take part in the further battle of the Nation. I beg the heads of the Armies, the Navy, and the Air

Force to strengthen by all possible means the spirit of resistance of our soldiers in the National-Socialist sense, with special reference to the fact that also I myself, as founder and creator of this movement, have preferred death to cowardly abdication or even capitulation.

May it, at some future time, become part of the code of honour of the German officer—as is already the case in our Navy—that the surrender of a district or of a town is impossible, and that above all the leaders here must march ahead as shining examples, faithfully fulfilling their duty unto death.

Second Part of the Political Testament

Before my death I expel the former Reichsmarschall Hermann Goering from the party and deprive him of all rights which he may enjoy by virtue of the decree of June 29th, 1941; and also by virtue of my statement in the Reichstag on September 1st, 1939, I appoint in his place Grossadmiral Doenitz, President of the Reich and Supreme Commander of the Armed Forces.

Before my death I expel the former Reichsfuehrer-SS and Minister of the Interior, Heinrich Himmler, from the party and from all offices of State. In his stead I appoint Gauleiter Karl Hanke as Reichsfuehrer-SS and Chief of the German Police, and Gauleiter Paul Giesler as Reich Minister of the Interior.

Goering and Himmler, quite apart from their disloyalty to my person, have done immeasurable harm to the country and the whole nation by secret negotiations with the enemy, which they conducted without my knowledge and against my wishes, and by illegally attempting to seize power in the State for themselves.

ADDENDUM C:

THEORETICAL DAMAGE TO PARIS FROM A 13-KILOTON ATOMIC BOMB DETONATED INSIDE THE LOUVRE
(Estimates from www.nuclearsecrecy.com)

There are approximately 730,000 people living in the area. About 100,000 would be killed, and another 240,000 injured. The weapon's fireball would be 240 yards wide; the air blast radius would extend almost 700 yards (the length of seven American football fields). The Louvre and all its contents would be incinerated and most other structures within this area (including Notre Dame Cathedral) would be demolished. Fatalities would be 100%.

Severe structural damage and heavy civilian casualties would extend more than one-half mile in all directions. Death from thermal burns and/or radiation poisoning would occur in a radius of one mile from ground zero. Lighter damage and injuries would extend as far out as two miles in all directions, and reach the Eiffel Tower, the Bastille, the Paris Observatory and Barbes. Damage to most of the art and cultural treasures of Paris would be catastrophic.

Northeastern prevailing winds would spread radioactive fallout 70 miles from Paris.

AUTHOR'S NOTE

The comments made by Benito Mussolini during his interview with the Italian journalist, Gian Gaetano Cabella, in the Palazzo Monforte, Milan, Italy, on Friday, April 20, 1945 are factual. Mussolini's interview was written off as the delusional raving of a doomed dictator. But it is a matter of record, and is included in many non-fiction World War II histories.

Incredibly, Giacomo and Lia De Maria, who put Mussolini and his mistress up while they were being detained by partisans shortly before their execution, did exist. As far as I have been able to determine, the couple, who owned a small farm near the Italian village of Giulino di Mezzagra, were apolitical. They probably had no choice in the matter. But they probably also acted out of simple Christian charity.

As noted, I share a last name with them, but no heritage. De Maria is a common name in Italy. My family originated in Sicily.

Also factual, although perhaps somewhat embellished, are meetings between Adolf Hitler and Albert Speer, and Speer and Walter Heisenberg.

The activities in the Führerbunker, and Martin Bormann's subsequent "escape" are a mix of fact and fiction, with more of the latter than the former. The same holds true for the fabrication of the Nazi A-bomb, which is, well, mostly fabrication (I hope!). The schematic of the bomb I have provided is also also a fabrication.

References to Nazi death camps and other atrocities are, of course, unfortunately based in fact. The truth of those bestialities is far worse than fiction. Patton did throw up when he visited the Orhdruff concentration camp.

The physics of the actual bomb is, unlike U-235, not pure. I made up some stuff, such as U-236 pollution. But the A-bomb dropped on Japan was almost exactly like the device I imagined in the Louvre.

How do I know? Well, you can get photos, schematics and instructions about the Hiroshima bomb, as well as the more-powerful Nagasaki plutonium bomb, on the Internet. In fact, you can also find out how H-bombs are made.

Have a good night's sleep.

***

We hope you will try all the author's books available on <u>Amazon</u>. He can be contacted at <u>ljdemaria@aol.com</u> or through his website, <u>www.lawrencedemaria.com</u>, and welcomes your comments.

<u>**ALTON RHODE MYSTERIES**</u>

<u>**JAKE SCARNE THRILLERS**</u>

<u>**COLE SUDDEN CIA THRILLERS**</u>

***

EXCERPTS FROM ALL THREE SERIES FOLLOW:

THE ALTON RHODE MYSTERY SERIES BEGAN WITH *CAPRIATI'S BLOOD*. HERE IS AN EXCERPT:

PROLOGUE

"They look smaller than the last bunch."

"You'll get more in the box," the elderly woman working the counter said. *"Same price. You can't beat it."*

"They taste the same?"

"If anything, they are sweeter." She pointed to a stand a few feet away. *"We have some free samples cut up over there. Try them."*

The man looked over at the table and saw that some flies hadn't needed an invitation.

"I'll take your word for it." His mother probably wouldn't know the difference. At least that was what he'd been told. The information had eased his conscience. Why risk a visit to someone who wouldn't even recognize her own son? But perhaps the occasional – and anonymous – gifts would soon be unnecessary. But just the thought of what he was going to do sent rivulets of sweat down the man's sides. *"What do I owe you?"*

"It comes to $34.95, shipping included east of the Mississippi."

Prices were going up on everything.

"Where's it going?"

The customer recited the address. Three times. Like everyone else in the goddamn town, the clerk *was a few years past her expiration date. That was one reason he was about to take the biggest risk of his life.*

"Want to include a card?"

"No."

"What's the return address?"

"If it doesn't get there," he said, smiling. "I don't want them back."

"I know, but we can apply a refund to your account."

"I don't have an account."

"It would be credited to your card. We take them all. American Express, MasterCard, Visa, Discover. Debit cards, too."

"I'm paying cash, don't worry about it."

"Well, if you give us your address, phone number and email, we can contact you."

He wanted to throttle the old crone. But long ago, for safety's sake, the man learned not to make a scene.

"No, thanks."

"We send out emails about our specials. People love them."

He took a deep breath and forced another smile. Then he pulled out his wallet and handed the woman $40.

"Just send the box. Keep the change."

*** *

It took the man an hour and a half to drive to Fort Lauderdale and settle in at the rundown motel off Dixie Highway straight out of the 1980's and run by a couple of Russians, which he thought was ironic considering what he was about to do. He registered using one of the many phony I.D.'s he'd collected over the years. They'd wanted a credit card at the desk "for incidentals," which from the look of the place might include pest control, but the extra hundred bucks he gave them along with the room charge he prepaid shut the Russkies up. They assumed he just wanted to get laid and didn't want to leave a paper trail. They were half right.

The call he planned to make on the room phone wasn't going to cost a hundred bucks. It would be short, sweet and to the point. A previous call, made a few days earlier from a similar dump in Sarasota, had insured that the lawyer would be in at 4 P.M. to take his call. The lawyer's secretary was a dim bulb but the mention that he had important information about the lawyer's main client finally sealed the deal.

The man looked at his watch. An hour to go. There was a bar across the street from the motel. He walked across and had three stiff bourbons. The last one barely managed to stop the tremor in his hand. One of the rummies sitting on a nearby stool smiled in commiseration. He pegs me as an alky like him, the man thought. He doesn't know I'm just scared shitless.

***

"It's that call you've been expecting, Mr. Rosenberg."

Samuel Rosenberg's secretary stood in the doorway to his office and could have announced the arrival of the Messiah with less fanfare. She was all of 22 and proof to him that the New York City public education system had gone into the toilet. He had tried to get her to use his first name and the phone intercom, with no luck on either.

Rosenberg sighed. She had only recently mastered the basic legal forms he rarely produced. His previous secretary was canned for running her mouth in the wrong places and the lawyer decided that if he had to choose between stupid and indiscreet, stupid was the way to go.

"Thank you, Francine," he said. "That's a fetching outfit you are wearing today."

She smiled and twirled away. Her clothes were still terrible, he knew, but at least they now covered her midriff. That was one battle won.

"This is Samuel Rosenberg," he said into the phone. He looked at the calendar on his desk for the name. "What can I do for you, er, Mr. Wagner?" He put his feet up on his desk and rocked back in his chair. "You mentioned something about one of my clients. I have many. Can you be more specific."

"Quit dicking around, counselor. You don't want me to be specific. We both know who we're talking about. I want you to be an intermediary between us. I have a proposal, a trade."

"I'm listening."

"I know who killed Fred Jarvis."

Rosenberg's feet came off the desk as he sat up. Like every attorney on Staten Island, he remembered the unsolved killing. Jarvis was a piece of crap, a

*crook, but a lawyer nonetheless. If crooked lawyers
became targets on Staten Island, who was safe?*

*"If it wasn't you," Rosenberg said coldly, "then I
suggest you contact the police. If you need
representation, I can suggest someone. What does
this have to do with my client?"*

*"Your client was with me. He saw everything,
too."*

*Jesus H. Christ. He reached for a pad and noted
the time, just because he felt he had to do something.
He looked at the caller I.D. It said "Unknown
Number."*

*"I thought that might get your attention. I guess
he forgot to mention it. We were young, and just
along for the ride, so to speak. Even so, we might
have been implicated as accessories. Not that we
were inclined to say anything back then. We were all
just one happy family. But things have changed. I
read the papers. He's got a shitpot of reasons why
he'd want the murder solved now, capische? He
would probably love to blow the whistle, but can't,
not without corroboration. So, here's the deal."*

*After the man finished speaking, Rosenberg said,
"I'll see what I can do."*

"It won't be easy, pal, there is a slight problem."
"What's that?"
"Your client wants to kill me."

***

*A half hour later Rosenberg pulled into the
Crooke's Point Marina in Great Kills Harbor. Not for
the first time he reflected that, considering who*

owned many of the boats docked there, the "e" could have been dropped from the marina's name.

Nando Carlucci was standing on the bridge of a Grady White whose engine was just then rumbling to life. Rosenberg climbed aboard clumsily. He didn't like boats, or fishing. But it was hard to bug a boat, especially when his client belonged to a boat club that allowed him the use of dozens of crafts of varying sizes on short notice. At least the Grady White was big enough to have an interior cabin. It really was cold. Ten minutes later he and Carlucci, the grossly overweight head of Staten Island's last remaining Italian crime family, were cruising a half mile offshore, far from any possible listening devices aimed their way. Yes, thank God for the Grady, Rosenbrg thought. Nando in anything smaller was an invitation to capsize.

"So, what the fuck is so urgent?"

The lawyer told him. Carlucci stared at him for a full minute.

"I can't believe the balls on the guy. After what he did to me. He's right, I'll kill him. What did he call himself?"

"Said his name was Wagner."

"Son of a bitch."

When Carlucci calmed down, he said, "What does he want?"

Rosenberg braced himself for another tirade.

"One million dollars and a head start after the trial."

Carlucci erupted again, flinging charts and ashtrays around the cabin. When he stopped, he said, "What do you think? Can you swing the deal?"

"I think so. It would be a feather in the D.A.'s cap. Can you swing the million?"

"Yeah, but tell him some of it has to be in jewelry, mostly diamonds."

Rosenberg didn't want to know where the jewelry was coming from. There had been a rash of burglaries in some of the borough's most upscale neighborhoods over the past few months. The cops were stumped, since some of the homes had state-of-the-art alarm systems. But the burglars vanished before the response cars arrived on the scene.

***

Wary at first, the D.A. and his assistants had grown more interested and animated as Carlucci and his lawyer outlined his plan in more detail during several secret meetings.

"We insist on full immunity for Mr. Carlucci," Rosenberg said, "as well as for the corroborating witness."

That had been the sticking point during the weeks of negotiations. The D.A. and his subordinates loathed Nando Carlucci. The idea of letting the fat mobster off the hook for a murder was repugnant to them.

"But you still won't tell us who this alleged witness is," one of the A.D.A's said.

"You don't have to know that now," Rosenberg said. "You have nothing to lose. We're the ones who *have to produce. Mr. Carlucci wants to do his civic duty and clear his conscience, even though he was but an innocent bystander in the lamentable affair."*

In the end, the D.A. went along with it.

"We'll get Carlucci eventually," he said after the meeting. "One big fish at a time."

As they drove away from the D.A.'s office, Rosenberg said, "I hope you know what you're doing, Nando. This is a big risk. Opens up a can of worms. He'd better produce."

"Don't you worry, counselor. He'll produce. He wants it bad."

"It's not just you, Nando. I've got my reputation to think of. My name will be anathema with the D.A. if we stiff him on this."

Carlucci looked at his lawyer with ill-concealed contempt.

"Your fuckin' name is an enema. You got no reputation to protect. Just do your job and wrap up the immunity thing tighter than a virgin's pussy. I don't have to remind you what happened to the last lawyer that fucked with my family, do I? That's how we got here, ain't it?"

***

CHAPTER 1 – THE RED LANTERN

Two Months Later

The workmen wheeled the last of the potted plant life into my office on hand dollies.

"You sure you don't want us to put some out in the reception area, Mr. Rhode?"

"I haven't finished painting it and the carpet is coming next week," I said. "I'd only have to move them all."

He shrugged and handed me an envelope.

"Miss Robart wrote down some instructions on how to care for them. She said if you have any questions, just call."

I'm not a plant guy. I'd keep the hardiest. The best shot at survival for the rest was my plan to donate them to other offices in the building. I called Nancy Robart at the Staten Island Botanical Garden to thank her for the foliage. She was the Executive Director and had donated the plants to give my new digs "some much needed class." She was at a luncheon, so I left the thank you on her voice mail.

Lunch sounded good to me. I opened a drawer in my desk, dropped Nancy's instructions in it and pulled out the holster containing my .38 Taurus Special. A lot of people in my line of work don't carry guns. Most of them have never been shot at, in war or peace. I have, in both, and like the comforting feel of iron on my hip. Besides, with all the hoops you have to jump through to get a permit in New York City (if you fill out the paperwork wrong they send you to Guantanamo), it seems silly not to carry. The Taurus revolver has only five chambers in its cylinder, to keep the weight down. But the bullets are big. The gun is meant for close-in work. Presumably if you need more than five shots a sixth won't matter.

I clipped the holster on my belt and shrugged into the brown corduroy jacket that was draped on the back of my chair. The jacket felt a little tight around the shoulders. I wasn't back to my old weight but my rehab, which included lifting iron, was redistributing muscle. I'd have to get my clothes altered soon. Or, assuming I got some clients, buy some new threads. But the jacket still fell nicely, even if it didn't quite cover the paint smudges on my jeans, and there was no gun bulge.

I walked down the stairs to the building lobby. The docs at the V.A. hospital said it would help strengthen my leg and it seemed to be working. The limp was barely noticeable. I stopped at the security station by the elevators and told the guard that I'd left my office unlocked because the cable company was scheduled to install my high-speed Internet and phone system sometime in the afternoon.

"You're the private eye on eight," she said. "Rhode." Her name tag said "H. Jones" and she was sturdily stout without being fat. Her skin color was only slightly darker than her tan uniform. "What time they give you?"

"Sometime between 1 PM and the next ice age," I said.

"I hear you." She wrote something in a large cloth-bound ledger, the kind that used to sit on hotel check-in counters and private eyes were able to read upside down in noir movies. I never could read upside down, so the move to hotel computers made no difference to me. "You coming back?"

"Yeah. Just running out to pick up some lunch."

"Where you headed?"

"Red Lantern, in Rosebank. You know it?"

"Oh, man. Best eggplant hero in the borough."

"Can I bring one back for you?"

"Sure."

She bent to get her purse.

"Forget it. My treat. What's the 'H' stand for?"

"Habika. It means 'sweetheart,' in some African language I have no clue about. My folks had just seen *Roots* when I was born. Coulda been worse, I guess."

"Alton," I said, extending my hand.

"Like I said, it coulda been worse," she said. "You can call me 'Abby'. Everyone else does. Abby Jones."

"Why not sweetheart, or sweetie?"

"Cause then I hit you upside your head. Listen, my brother works at the cable company. I'll give him a call to make sure they don't forget about you."

A Rhode rule: It never hurts to buy an eggplant hero for a security guard.

There was a bank branch in the lobby. It had an ATM but the daily limit was $400 and I had a bar tab to square. I was working off the cash from a dwindling home equity line of credit inexplicably approved by the same bank. I wondered if I could be nailed for trading on inside information if I shorted its stock because it lent me the money.

The branch manager came out of his cubbyhole to shake my hand, smiling effusively. He led me over to a cute little redhead teller who thanked me before,

233

during and after the transaction. If I'd wanted a toaster, she would have gone home and taken one from her own kitchen. The banks had a lot of PR ground to make up.

I now had a grand in my pocket. Flush and hungry; a combination that always works for me. I planned to walk the mile or so along Bay Street to the Red Lantern. But it was drizzling, with the imminent promise of something heavier. With a corduroy jacket I'd weigh as much as Donald Trump's hairdo by the time I arrived. I don't use an umbrella unless animals are lining up two-by-two on the ark ramp.

My three-year old light blue Chevy Malibu is distinguished only by several round indentations on its trunk and rear panels. I'd bought it at Honest Al Lambert's Used Car Lot in Tottenville. Al had acquired six almost-pristine Malibus at auction from a rental fleet, but hadn't counted on the car carrier transporting them from Denver running into a vicious hail storm in Indiana. The vehicles on top had their windshields smashed and their bodywork turned into the far side of the moon. Undaunted, Al tried to sell me one of those. But even the dimmest suspect might notice being followed by a car with more dimples than a golf ball. So, I opted for one of the Malibus on the carrier's first level, which sustained little damage but were still heavily discounted. It looked like every third car on the road. Still, I made a few modifications, including a passenger-side ejector seat activated by a red button hidden in the gear shift. I didn't actually do that.

At the Red Lantern all the parking spots, including those next to fire hydrants, bus stops and "No Parking" signs, were filled with cars that had official stickers or emblems: police, fire, sanitation, court officers, judges, Borough Hall, Coast Guard. Coast Guard? The NFL season was in full swing. It was Friday and the regular lunchtime crowd was inflated by dozens of people dropping off betting slips for Sunday's games in the bar's huge football pool. My glove compartment was full of phony decals and emblems that I would have used in an illegal spot if one was available, but I couldn't chance double parking and blocking in some Supreme Court judge. I settled for a spot two blocks away.

This section of Rosebank, once almost exclusively Italian, with a sprinkling of Jewish delis and bakeries, now had businesses run by more recent immigrants. I passed a Korean nail salon flanked by an Indian restaurant and a Pakistani convenience store. Across the street was something called the Somali-American Social Club, where a tall man in a white dashiki stood outside smoking. Probably didn't want to light up inside near the explosives. Two doors down, Gottleib's Bakery, a local institution for 80 years, still held the fort. If World War III broke out, I was pretty certain it would start here.

Inside the Red, patrons were two-deep at the rail keeping three bartenders hopping. All the tables in the front and back rooms were occupied and I pushed my way to the bar. The front room had dimpled tin ceilings that tended to amplify and redirect noise. In fact, because of an acoustic anomaly, something said at one end of the bar might be heard clearly at the other end. Of course, most conversations were lost in the mix of babble, but people still tended to be discreet. If you wanted to ask for a quick blow job in the car, or you were a city councilman asking five large in cash from a contractor who needed a zoning variance, you might as well put it on cable. The half-oval bar ran the length of the front room and had a dark green leather border matched by the upholstery of high-back swivel stools. A large silver trophy depicting a crouching man with his hand swept back occupied a place of honor next to the register. Its nameplate read "R. Kane." Underneath that, "1973 Tri-State Handball Championships." A third line said "Second Place."

Roscoe Kane, 60 pounds past his handball prime, lumbered over. I reached in my pocket, counted off $500 and put it on the bar.

"Take me off the books."

"Business picking up?"

"I'm being optimistic."

Reaching behind the register, Roscoe pulled out a beat-up marble notebook of the type your mother bought for your first day of school. He laid it on the bar, flipped some pages, picked up a pencil and crossed something out. He took $420 from the pile and put it in the cash drawer. At the same time, he reached down into a cooler, lifted out a bottle of Sam Adams Light, twisted off the cap with one hand and slid it down to me. Ex-handball champs don't lack for manual dexterity. He put the notebook away. I knew that dozens, maybe hundreds, of similar notebooks had served the same purpose since the Red Lantern, one of the oldest taverns in the city, opened its doors back when the Kings Rifles garrisoned Staten Island.

Roscoe put some bar nuts in front of me and said, "Glass? Lunch?"

"No, and yes," I said through a mouthful of nuts. "Two eggplant heroes to go."

I took a long draw on my beer. It was ice cold. Not too many people drank Sam Adams in the Red, let alone Sam Adams Light, but Roscoe kept in a stash for me. It was the only light beer I'd ever had that didn't taste light.

I said, "Is it true that the Algonquins ran a tab in here?"

"Never. Bastards stiffed us."

"Yeah," one of the regulars at the bar snorted, "and this place hasn't bought back a drink since."

As I sipped my beer, I turned to scan the opposite wall, which was covered floor to ceiling with tally sheets for the 1,400 people in the football pool. The alphabetically-listed entrants were a democratic cross section of the populace, including just about every elected and appointed official, several judges, a smattering of assistant district attorneys, college professors, scores of cops and half the hoods in the borough. The sheets were taken down after the Monday night games and updated by the three elderly Italian ladies who also ran the kitchen. No one questioned their cooking or their accuracy.

I felt a blast of chilly air. The bar's cheerful hubbub eased a bit and one of the other bartenders said "shit" under his breath. I turned as Arman Rahm and a fire hydrant entered the bar. The fire hydrant's name was Maks Kalugin and had more bullet holes in him than Emperor Maximilian.

***

NEXT:

THE FIRST OF THE JAKE SCARNE THRILLER SERIES, IN FACT, THE FIRST OF DE MARIA'S NOVELS, IS *SOUND OF BLOOD*. HERE IS A SAMPLE:

CHAPTER 1 – DANGEROUS MARINE ORGANISMS

"Can't we shoot him?"

"What?"

"Just once, let's just shoot someone," Keitel shouted in frustration, as well as to be heard over the growling engine. "Or strangle him."

The outboard was the proximate source of his anger.

"How about a knife? I'm wonderful with a knife. Good with bombs, too. We could blow up his ridiculous car." He leaned precariously over the stern to untangle the cast net from the cowling, where it threatened to foul a propeller. "Somebody should." The net came loose suddenly and Keitel fell hard on his rump. His already abused coccyx throbbed with a pain reminiscent of bad landings in his paratroop days. He let out a string of curses in German, a sure sign of rage. "Why must everything be such a production?"

The 24-foot Dusky was pitching badly in the shallows off Sunny Isles beach. The man at the wheel glanced toward the shore 100 feet away. An old woman shooing children out of the water gave him the fish eye. Jesús Garza feared few things. A Cuban abuela protecting her brood was one. They didn't need more problems. He and Christian were behind schedule; the light was going. So while he enjoyed Keitel's discomfort immensely, Garza gently throttled back the small sport fishing boat and gave the woman a friendly wave. Unmollified, she continued to direct a baleful glare at him. Christ, he thought, she could stop global warming with that look.

"This whole plan is the product of a deranged mind," Keitel groused. He was angrily refolding the dripping net. "Fucking *Pirates of the Caribbean!*"

"Watch your language. The wind is blowing toward shore. The children may hear you. Might I suggest you try hitting the water? There is an awful lot of it and we already have an engine."

"The hell with the children," Keitel said. But he lowered his voice.

Garza grinned broadly as his partner struggled with his footing. Shorter than his lean, angular friend, with a welterweight's balance and build, he had sturdy sea legs. Keitel, stubbornly ignoring the offer of a seat cushion, had taken the brunt of the bouncy ride up from the Key Biscayne marina. Cruising back and forth along Miami Beach for two hours in heavy chop before finding a patch of the slimy buggers had been no picnic either, Garza knew. They should have opted for the bigger Dusky with its twin 225 Evinrudes. He laughed. Christian could catch a bigger motor.

"I'm glad you find all this humorous," Keitel said.

"You're bunching it too tightly. Remember the video."

Both men had watched a homemade Internet tutorial on how to throw a cast net. The redneck fisherman in the video had a belly the size of a beluga whale but looked like Nureyev when throwing the net.

"It's not that easy, you idiot," Keitel snarled. "The expert fisherman! Salt water in your veins. You try it." He prided himself in his ability to hit whatever he aimed at. Missing the Atlantic Ocean was inconceivable.

"Then who would handle the boat? If you were up here, we'd be in Mindel's parking lot. No, today you are first mate, and barely passable at that."

"Eat a turd. Mindel's isn't even there anymore. He sold to a developer."

"Pity. I was quite fond of the pastrami and the pickle plate."

"And I'm fond of my spine." Water splashed over the gunwale and Keitel used a muscled forearm to brush blonde hair out of his eyes. "Did you have to hit every damn wave on the way here?"

***

If folded properly – and loosely – across one arm and thrown with a whirling bodily motion, a cast net, lined with dozens of small lead balls, opens into a circle before hitting the water. A good cast has a lot in common with a golf swing. Less effort typically produces better results. A hard toss usually leads to a clumped net. The thick gloves didn't help. They caught in the webbing. Most of Keitel's casts hadn't even cleared the boat. The most recent one did manage to clear the stern but didn't quite get past the engine.

But he finally got the hang of it and even managed to impart some savoir faire to the endeavor. Gradually his mood improved. After one ballet-like cast, he bowed to Garza's applause. The eighth toss was particularly fruitful, and he did a count after adding the contents to the live well.

"Ten or eleven, I think. It's hard to be sure. Enough?"

"For a Cape Buffalo. Dump the net and wash your gloves. Keep them on."

Garza waited until Keitel sat – this time on two cushions, he noted – and opened the throttle, heading south past Bal harbor and Surfside. A few minutes later he slowed near the familiar high rise and reached for his binoculars.

"There he is," he said, cutting the engine just off a sandbar at 63rd Street.

As Keitel dropped anchor he glanced toward shore, where a surfcaster wading knee-deep in the water was expertly flicking his bait just short of a sandbar. The setting sun was blocked by the condo building and this section of beach was in deep shade. The few people still stretched out on blankets would soon depart. A bronzed old man with a metal detector scoured the sand nearby, his rhythmic sweeps regular as a metronome. Garza went to the stern, opened a Styrofoam cooler and pulled out a large white plastic bag. He leaned over the side and partially filled the bag with seawater. After testing the bag's strength and integrity by jouncing it several times, he reached in the cooler for a long-handled kitchen strainer and a pair of gloves. Then he peered into the well.

"What do you think? Intelligent design or evolution? I can argue either."

"I'm sure you could," Keitel said. "You always do. As if it matters."

"Christian, I'm always amazed at your lack of intellectual curiosity. Are you not interested in the wonders of creation and the universe we inhabit? You hail from a country that produced Einstein for God's sake."

"My universe is centered on my throbbing ass. And Einstein was a Jew."

"Do I detect anti-Semitism in that remark? I'm shocked."

"I'm no anti-Semite. You know I worked with the Mossad against the Syrians. That's how I met Lev. I know I told you about him."

Indeed he had, Garza thought, with the usual twinge of jealousy. He was sorry he brought up the damn subject at all. Keitel never missed a chance to mention his one-time Israeli commando boyfriend. The Israeli Defense Force was very open- minded. It didn't matter if you enjoyed screwing camels, as long as you also enjoyed killing Arabs.

"Gave me a commendation," Keitel continued. He saw the expression on Garza's face. "I know. Jews giving German soldiers medals. Crazy. Hitler was a fool. Should have made peace with the Jews instead of driving them into the hands of his enemies. The Nazis would have gotten the bomb. The world would be speaking German. Like all fanatics, he had limited vision."

"Thank God. German is too difficult a language. But I am impressed with your reasoning. I may have to reevaluate my opinion of you."

"Reevaluate my dick and impress me with your silence. Let's do this."

"All right, if you insist. Hold the bag open. Wide open."

***

A rare December gale, far at sea, was roiling the shelf water. Breakers crashed over sand bars 30 yards out. By now the surfcaster could hear more than see them. But the phosphorescent foam told him they were substantial. So did the smell. The agitated water released the sea's essence, an intoxicating mixture of brine, minerals, seaweed, marine life – and death. A wave swelled up to the fisherman's waist. There was a splash of spray and the taste of salty spindrift on his lips. Something stuck to his cheek and his heart fluttered. A tendril came away in his hand. But it was all right; it was green. The wind-driven surf was pushing seaweed and flotsam toward land. By morning the beach would be rife with coral, sponges and sea fans, which local shore rats would sell to tourists for beer and butt money. From a distance the gunk piled at the tide line would look like a Normandy hedgerow.

The on-shore wind also brought the danger of the beautiful but toxic Portuguese Men-of-War. The distinctive dark blue "sail" that gave the little jellyfish their name caught the breeze and sent them toward land. At certain times of the year – this was one of them – hundreds of Men-of-War would be left high and dry by the receding tide. Their tentacles remained vital even when drying out. The little "bluebottles" attracted the curious, particularly children, and the fisherman always made a point of warning them.

He hadn't really thought the strand on his face was a tentacle, but the stab of fear was instinctive. Weeks earlier, also while wading, his right calf had exploded in pain, as if slashed with a hot razor. The agony shot to his groin; he thought he was in real trouble. After scraping the four-inch tentacle off his leg with sand and seawater, he limped back to his apartment and washed the affected area with vinegar, one of several home remedies purported to neutralize jellyfish venom. (Another is urine, but pissing on demand was never one of his strong suits.) The throbbing remained intense and he finally went to Flagler General.

"The groin pain just radiated up a nerve," the emergency room doctor told him after giving him a shot. "Allergic reactions to jellyfish are rare. Your throat would swell and you'd have trouble breathing. The real danger is cardiac arrest caused by shock when a huge dose of toxin hits near the heart or head. But one bluebottle isn't going to do it. A box jellyfish, maybe, but this isn't Australia. Of course, now that you've been sensitized, your next reaction might be different."

With that warning in mind, before fishing he looked to see if the aptly named blue "Dangerous Marine Organisms" flags were flying from the rescue shacks and kept a cell phone handy in his bucket. This wasn't South Beach; after dark he would be alone. Half the condos were vacant, owned by now-desperate speculators. Until the sun set, his main company had been the ubiquitous sandpipers pecking like typists on the keyboard of the shore and brown pelicans skimming the waves. There seemed to be more pelicans than usual. The fisherman wondered if some of them were refugees from the oil spill in the Gulf that had somehow traversed the Florida peninsula, or had been cleaned in the Panhandle and relocated. Then again, the mind saw what it wanted to see. Everyone in the country had pelicans on the brain. But he would check it out. Could be a great story.

As it darkened, all the birds flew off to wherever birds go at night. The only humans around were a couple of diehard bathers and an old man with a metal detector who, as he passed the fisherman, gave him a "me neither" shrug. There were also two men on a fishing boat just past the bars. Curious. Most small craft anchored further out, in calmer water. A man at the wheel swept the beachfront with binoculars, probably looking at a few skimpily clad women on the pool decks of nearby hotels.

***

The prospector and bathers were gone, and the surfcaster could no longer see the boat. He didn't mind. New-found anonymity and Florida's milder climate provided a solitude he'd craved in New York. He religiously broke up his work week by fishing this stretch of beach every Wednesday. He'd even delayed his research trip to Antigua by a day so as not to break his routine.

A routine that had not gone unnoticed.

***

What we do with a drunken sailor?
What we do with a drunken sailor, early in the morning?

"Jesus, Jesús, not only can't you sing," an exasperated Keitel said as he lifted the plastic bag from the live well, "but the words are wrong."

Garza was undeterred by the criticism of his sea chanty.

"Cuban version. And look who's the music expert," he said. "The only song you know is *Deutschland Uber Alles*."

Keitel laughed and gave the bag a few hard shakes to test its integrity.

"It will hold. Are you sure it's dark enough?"

"Yes. You can see nothing from the buildings. Same moon as last night."

"I'll do it if you want," Keitel said quietly. "I'm the better swimmer."

Garza was touched. Christian was always full of surprises.

"Your heart isn't in it. And as you ungraciously reminded me, this is my lunatic idea. But I appreciate the gesture."

Slipping over the side, Garza found that he could almost stand. Keitel reached over the gunwale and handed him the tightly-tied plastic bag, holding it gingerly by its drawstring, which he wrapped around his partner's wrist.

"Buena suerta," Keitel said.

Garza smiled. The online language classes were obviously working.

"Danke."

He started side-stroking toward shore at a slight angle. As he disappeared from sight, Keitel could hear him singing happily.

Fifteen men on a dead man's chest, Yo ho ho and a bottle of rum...

***

The turbulent surf was a smorgasbord of organic matter and small crustaceans. That attracted baitfish, pilchards and silversides, whose sole purpose was to occupy low rungs in the food chain, where they provided a moveable feast for larger predators: small sharks, bluefish, barracuda, jacks and pompano.

There was too much seaweed to use lures, so the fisherman baited his hook with a chunk of herring, to which he attached a strip of squid. Both had been purchased, rather guiltily, at a nearby Publix; he hadn't had time to go to the marina. Well, he mused, one man's sushi was another man's bait. He felt a sharp jab on his ankle. Reaching down he brought up a large, faded conch shell. He was tempted to put it to his ear but recalled a recent run-in with a hermit crab that had taken up residence in another conch. The cheeky little devil nipped his lobe in annoyance. It wasn't even the crab's own shell! He'd tell Emma the story when she visited. She'd get a kick out of it. He smiled as the thought of her brought back a memory from their shared childhood, another beach, another shell – the first time he'd crossed swords with his uncle. But certainly not the last. Just wait until the old reprobate gets a load of what …

The rod tip jerked, and the reel's drag started clicking wildly. The fisherman flipped the nondescript conch away (there were many more colorful specimens in his collection) and set the hook, using a wave to surf the seaweed-covered fish the final few feet. A bluefish flopped helplessly in the sand. It was small, maybe three pounds, with a streamlined body built for speed and a piranha-like head. The analogy was apt. Feeding blues easily topped the ferocity of the much smaller Amazon denizens and had even been known to bite bathers in their blood lust. The unfortunate bluefish suffocating on the beach was certainly not alone. Blues travel in schools of like-sized fish. If it was one of the smaller blues in its pod, he might get a five or six pounder! He dumped the flopping fish in the ice-filled bag inside his bucket, in his excitement receiving several nasty finger cuts from its razor-sharp teeth. He rebaited quickly. The type of bait at this point was academic. Blues chomp anything. He could have saved money and bought a package of hot dogs.

The next cast went into a trough only 20 feet from shore where a platoon of blues from a larger school swirled under the seaweed. Eventually they would head to deep water to rejoin the main pod, guided by senses that could detect a single drop of blood in a cubic acre of water. A savage hit! This blue ripped off line. He tightened the drag and worked the frantic fish back. Eventually it tired. A beauty, at least five pounds. He shoved the blue into his bag, where it thrashed violently against its deceased cousin. He would keep both. Blues this size tasted like real fish, not the sauced-up slabs of Chilean sea bass or tilapia passed off as haute cuisine in the tourist traps on Lincoln Road. And what the hell was monkfish? He bent down to cut more bait.

"Catch anything?"

Startled, he nearly baited his finger. He whirled around, dropping his knife in the sand. A man stood beside him holding a large plastic bag.

"Jesus, you almost gave me a cardiac!"

"To be quite accurate, it's Jesús," the man said, smiling. "I'm sorry." He didn't seem sorry. "I was swimming and saw you. I fish."

Slight accent, probably Cuban. Good-looking, with a small black mustache that matched his slick, jet-black hair. He looked like one of the rhumba dancers on a cruise ship. Beaded with water, the stranger wore a tight black bathing suit that boldly outlined his genitals. At his hip was a small waterproof pouch. Rubber gloves were tucked into the other side of the suit. The plastic bag looked half full, with a watery luminescence. The man carefully placed it on the sand. Liquid spilled from the neck, and a strand of … something … slithered out. He opened his pouch and took out a cigarette. He did not offer one to the fisherman and took quite some time with a lighter, flicking it on and off several times before lighting the cigarette.

"These things will kill you," he said, laughing at some private joke as smoke hissed from his nostrils.

The fisherman heard a motor start up, and then a muted throbbing. He looked toward his apartment house, barely visible 200 feet away. There were lights in the high rise and on a calmer day he would have been able to hear the hum of traffic on Collins Avenue. But not tonight. The stranger's appearance unnerved him. This section of Miami Beach was in transition and just north Collins still had its fair share of cheap convenience stores, coffee shops, payday loan operations, burger and burrito joints with vinyl chairs, seedy beach bars and vagrants. This man was no vagrant, but that was small comfort. It's not easy to look sinister in a bathing suit, but the stranger managed it.

There was a thump as a fish tail flapped out of the bucket.

"Ah, bluefish," the stranger said, peering in. "They'll be delicious. How would you have prepared them?"

The fisherman relaxed, not noting the phrasing.

"I like to marinate them in key lime juice and dark rum. Then dust them with a little flower and bake then at 400 degrees. Maybe 10 minutes."

He was about to suggest an appropriate wine when the "Cuban" looked past his shoulder out to sea and said loudly, "He's alone. No one in either direction." He flicked away his cigarette and put on the gloves.

A clipped voice behind the fisherman said, "Make it quick."

He turned to see another man walking from the ocean. Sensing danger, he reached down to grab the knife, sticking hilt up in the sand. Too late. Garza lifted the plastic bag and in one practiced motion flipped it over the fisherman's head, pulling the drawstring taut. Seawater and slime fill the man's nostrils and ears. The seal wasn't perfect and most of the water gushed out the bottom of the bag, leaving only the congealed "things" that had been floating inside. Something in the fisherman's midbrain, just barely below the level of consciousness, a genetic remnant of primate fear, recognized the creatures. Although slimy, they seemed to be attaching themselves to his face.

Jellyfish! Something twirled up his nose. He dropped his knife as his hands flew up. He barely hooked his thumbs under the throat of the bag when dozens of tentacles almost simultaneously discharged their poison. It felt like scalding water. His eyeballs exploded. He inhaled reflexively to scream and the fire filled his esophagus, which closed in an agonizing spasm. The fisherman pitched backwards into the sand near the waterline, limbs twitching uncontrollably. Then he went limp, hooded head rolling freely in the waves.

Keitel reached into the dead man's bucket and pulled out a ziplock bag. "Keys, wallet and cell phone," he said. "Convenient."

Then the killers each grabbed the corpse by an arm and started to drag it into the ocean.

"Wait," said Garza, dropping one arm, which started flopping grotesquely in the surf. He went to the bucket and retrieved the bag with the night's catch.

"Are you completely insane?"

"I like bluefish," Garza said. "He gave me a great recipe."

Once in the water, they flipped their victim over and then paddled him out to the boat, face down. No harm in being sure. After climbing into the Dusky, they carefully removed the fatal hood from the fisherman, whose bulging, spider-veined eyes stared at them in seeming reproach. The jellyfish slid into the water, but some blue, beaded strands remained attached to the dead man's face. Tendrils twirled out from his nose and covered his upper lip.

"He looks like Salvador Dali," Keitel observed.

"That's not a good look for him," Garza said. He gave the body a gentle, almost loving, push towards shore. "Now he belongs to the algae," he intoned solemnly. They had recently watched a History

Channel special about the Lincoln assassination. "Get it?"

"It's not funny when you have to explain it," Keitel said.

Garza reached into his pouch and lit a cigarette, which he needed a lot more than the one he used on the beach as a signal. The corpse slowly sank from sight. The man had to be found. A mysterious disappearance might spur an open-ended inquiry. The body would wash ashore, but only after the sea and its creatures muddied the forensic waters. There would be no signs of man-made trauma. It was a murder using only natural ingredients.

"You know, Christian, Greenpeace would be proud of us."

"What are you talking about?"

"Never mind. Take the wheel. I'll put lures on the rods. We should look the part when we get back to the dock. Hell, we even have some fish."

He lifted the top of a seat and pulled out a tackle box. He knew what he was doing. As a boy in Cuba he fished the Guantanamo River with his father and uncles, near where the big waterway ran to the sea, splitting the now infamous American naval base in two. They often came so close to the base perimeter that Marine sentries fishing from the bulkhead waved. The perimeter searchlights, designed to spot intruders – mostly Cubans swimming to freedom – were an irresistible magnet to huge shrimp, which the marines put on hooks.

"You wouldn't believe it, Chico," his father told him, "they get big jacks, tarpon, barracuda, because of those lights. I saw a 100-pound tarpon, a five-footer, leap like a sardine. Even the Marines jumped back. Then we saw the big shadow in the water. Tiburòn, a hammerhead. Chasing the tarpon. At least 15 feet and 2,000 kilos! Eyes this far apart." His father held his arms as wide as he could. He was a fisherman, after all. "Only a fool would swim there."

Another time, he tried to step on a log jutting from shore. The "log" turned out to be a giant barracuda. Huge eyes rolled up to look at his foot, which he held in midair as his shaken father snatched him back and hugged him tight. And he recalled how he his uncles passed him the rum bottle after a manta ray big as a Piper Cub jumped over their boat. What fun they had! Garza felt a twinge of remorse. His father would not have liked him killing a fisherman.

Christian was saying something.

"You should call them. Are you listening? You're a thousand miles away."

"Only 90," Garza said, picking up his cell phone from a bag at his feet.

***

In a luxurious penthouse in Coral Gables, a man teetered at his climax. The woman astride him was motionless but for the slight rise and fall of a small blue tattoo at the base of her spine as she clenched her internal sexual muscles. She had brought the moaning man close several times. Now she would end the sublime torture. She had a reservation at Joe's Stone

255

Crabs. Not with him. A cell phone buzzed on the side table.

"Fuck! Leave it alone," the man gasped. "I'm almost there."

The woman climbed off. The man cursed and squirmed, all he could do with hands tied to the bedposts. She placed the phone to the man's ear.

"Yes," he gasped. "Wha… What is it?" He listened. "OK. OK. Fine."

The woman threw the phone on the table. Her face was expressionless.

"Well?"

"It's done," he replied, groaning as she remounted.

"One less thing for us to worry about. Any problems?"

"For the love of God, can we talk about it later?"

"We both agreed on this. Perhaps I should get these things in writing."

"I'll sign the goddamn Magna Carta if you want! Let's talk about it later!"

She laughed. The tattoo, of the Cross of Lorraine, resumed its rhythmic pulsation. She increased the frequency. A moment later her pinioned partner bucked upward violently, roaring in release. She gazed down at him dispassionately as his breathing slowly returned to normal and his eyes began to refocus. He could never be bored with her. That was the problem with all the men she slept with. True, he had been the most interesting. An affair that started with attempted rape had evolved into a lustful

256

business relationship (in her mind, the best kind of sex). But she was ready to move on. They would still need each other, of course. There was a company to run. She wondered how he'd take it. Probably not well.

He was trying to say something.

"Shhhh, darling" she said, putting a finger to his lips. "Be right with you."

Her hips began to move slowly. The pace quickened. Her mouth opened and her head tilted back, throat taut. A flush spread across her breasts. Their nipples, always prominent, became rock hard. A series of guttural cries. A final shudder. Her face softened into a smile. The man was mesmerized, as always. It was like watching a swaying cobra.

***

"What did he say?"

"He couldn't talk." Garza laughed. "He was tied up."

He remembered the fisherman's wallet. The apartment and car would be sanitized but people kept important information on their person: locker and safety deposit numbers, even computer passwords. Using a penlight he went through the billfold and was mildly surprised to find several crisp $100 bills, which he happily pocketed. There were a half dozen credit cards. One in particular stood out.

"I thought this guy was a struggling journalist."

"That's what they told me," Keitel said. "Why?"

"He's got a Titanium American Express card."

"So?"

Garza didn't bother to explain. Christian left money matters to him. He wouldn't know a Titanium card meant its owner had a net worth of at least $10 million. He pulled the card out of its sleeve and read the name. Confused, he scanned the driver's license.

"Son of a bitch."

He reached for his cell phone.

***

Luke Goldfarb had a problem most 14-year-old boys only dreamed about. The three girls on the adjacent blanket were topless. That wasn't the problem. Unlike his grandparents, who looked like raisins after 30 years in Miami Beach, Luke, down from New York for a visit, was turning into the world's largest blister. He needed the umbrella that was back in the condo. His grandparents were out shopping for Hanukkah. Before the girls took off their bikini tops, Luke's thoughts had revolved around homemade sufganiyot – jelly donuts. Now all he wanted was to plant that umbrella like the Marines on Iwo Jima. *I love you, Nana and Gramps, but I hope the engine falls out of your Escallade.* He took a few deep breaths, thought about the Knicks to quell his erection and started to get up. Just then, the girls also stood and headed toward the ocean. Luke followed. Soon all four were standing side by side waist deep.

"Look at that," one girl said. For a horrible moment, Luke, embarrassingly aware of his excitement, thought he wasn't in deep enough. But then he followed her finger and saw something dark silhouetted by a wave. It was big.

258

"Probably a dolphin," he squeaked, unforgivably. He had never spoken to a half-naked girl, let alone three. "Maybe a sand shark," he was able to croak.

Luke thought that they would scurry to shore. He would stand his ground to impress them, although he did feel a thrill of fear. But these were Florida girls and edged out toward the object. It didn't look like a fish. A log? He was about to tell them to be careful when the wave rolled the object right into the girls. All erotic thoughts were blown out of his mind as they screamed and ran. He swore later that the tits on the middle girl, the one with the large, dark aureoles, "twirled" in opposite directions like a New Year's Eve party favor. It was sight Luke Goldfarb would remember the rest of his life, second only to the naked, bloated, almost faceless corpse now bumping gently against his hip.

* * *

NEXT:

THE FIRST OF THE COLE SUDDEN C.I.A. THRILLER SERIES WAS *SUDDEN KILL*. HERE IS A SAMPLE:

CHAPTER 1 – A LIVE ONE

The four bull sharks circled below the strange-looking raft bobbing in the gentle swells amid smaller pieces of flotsam.

Bull sharks are found worldwide, most commonly near shores. They prefer the shallows, but they are tough, adaptive animals, especially when hungry, and often travel far up rivers (among their many attributes is the fact that they can thrive in fresh water). Bull sharks have been found in the Mississippi all the way into Illinois.

They derive their name from their stocky shape and broad, flat snout, as well as their aggressive behavior. Normally solitary hunters, they will only occasionally pair up to corral prey. Thus, this toothsome quartet was highly unusual. Their atypical behavior may have been precipitated by the chaos inflicted on the Gulf of Mexico and its denizens by the huge hurricane that had just passed through.

Vicious, unpredictable predators, bull sharks are responsible for many of attacks on humans attributed to other sharks, particularly the Great White. Many scientists now believe that bull sharks, and not a Great White, were responsible for the rash of deadly attacks along the New Jersey coast in 1916 that inspired the book and movie, *Jaws*. While they don't specifically target humans, bull sharks will go anywhere in search of a meal. Bulls have been known to swim through the streets of flooded coastal cities.

They are not picky eaters. Floating bodies are a favored treat.

The smallest of the group beneath the raft was a seven-footer. Occasionally one of them closed on the raft and slammed into it. They had been at it a long time and would have stayed indefinitely, drawn by the steady seep of blood and other organic fluids that drifted down from the raft.

It was a human chum line no shark could resist.

Suddenly a huge shadow came between the circling sharks and the raft above. The massive creature glided down toward them. The bull sharks, with millions of years of accumulated instinct, recognized its malevolent intent.

The bulls scattered. They had been looking for a meal, not auditioning to become one.

Whatever was on the raft now belonged to a much bigger shark.

A hammerhead.

***

Commander Bret Pagano knew he was pushing it. The MH-60T Jayhawk had barely enough fuel to make it back to the crew's base in Sarasota. Of course, in a pinch he could set down safely anywhere along the devastated Florida coast. But that probably wouldn't help any survivors they might find who were in bad shape.

Besides, his crew needed rest. And, he admitted, so did he. They had been running double and triple missions for three days. A replacement team waiting in Sarasota would be sharper – a consideration more important than pride when lives were at stake.

Not that this crew wanted to rest. The previous day they had rescued a dozen people drifting in the Gulf, including several children. They were still on an adrenaline and emotional high. The Coast Guard lived to save lives. Its men and women breathed the Coast Guard motto they all memorized in training: *I serve the people of the United States. I will protect them. I will defend them. I will save them. I am their shield.*

Pagano smiled at the thought of the service's unofficial motto: *You have to go out, but you don't have to come back!* It dated to an 1899 United States Lifesaving Service regulation, which states that Coast Guard personnel must persevere "in attempting a rescue" until "the impossibility of effecting a rescue is demonstrated."

That led to many near-suicidal assignments, in all sorts of weather. The old regulation, he knew, didn't speculate on what might happen to the rescuers.

Pagano looked down at the Gulf of Mexico, unnaturally calm after the hurricane.

Still ….

"Let's call it a day, Meg."

"Roger, Skipper."

It had not taken Pagano very long to get used to having a woman as a co-pilot, or to find out that on any given day she could fly rings around him. That was three years ago. Lieutenant Margaret O'Malley would soon have her own bird. He'd miss her competence and good cheer.

Pagano started to pull on the yoke. A shower, hot chow and some rack time was just what the doctor ordered.

Then he spotted something on the horizon.

***

The young Airman scanning the Gulf from the chopper door was on his first "combat" assignment. Having survived the Coast Guard's rigorous para-rescue training school, with its 70 percent washout rate, his trial by fire, or rather, water, had quickly solidified his standing with his older flight mates, both officer and enlisted. They had teased him about his eagerness to jump out of the hovering copter to save someone.

"Only over water, son," his Flight Mechanic crew chief had said, only half joking.

It was the young Airman's first hurricane – he was from Minnesota – and he never wanted to see another. The stretch of southwest Florida coast they were searching was devastated. Some areas looked like a bomb or tornado had hit. Not all of the victims the crew eventually unloaded to waiting hospitals were alive. But enough were, so he didn't care how long the pilot kept the chopper in the air.

He'd follow his skipper right into the drink if he'd asked.

The helicopter tilted slightly and began a gradual turn. The crew chief moved to his side and said, "Skipper is calling it a day. We're heading back."

The Airman gave him a thumbs-up but kept his eyes on the expanse of water below. You never knew.

***

"What's that down there, Chief?"

The older man leaned out the door past the Airman to get a better look. The sea was littered with debris, much of it small.

"Don't know."

He started to key his helmet mike when the chopper tilted and made a sharp turn, quickly lost altitude and headed toward the area that had caught their attention.

"Skipper saw it," the Chief said. "Got eyes like an osprey."

A minute later they were hovering above the object.

"Looks like a roof of some sort," the Airman said. "Is that a man?"

"Sure is," the Chief said.

Despite 20 years with the Coast Guard, he was still excited every time they found a live one.

"Get the hoist and basket ready."

"What's that next to him?"

The pilot skillfully hovered the copter 25 feet above the target. The Chief peered down.

"Son of a bitch," he said. "Kid, that's not something you see every day."

Available on Amazon (e-books and print):

THE JAKE SCARNE THRILLERS

SOUND OF BLOOD

MADMAN'S THIRST

KILLERFEST

THE VIRON CONSPIRACY

PEDESTAL

FACETS

CHANCE

THE ALTON RHODE MYSTERIES

CAPRIATI'S BLOOD

LAURA LEE

SIREN'S TEARS

SISTER

GUNNER

THE ELSON LEGACY

TURTLE DOVE

SHADOW OF THE BLACK WOMB

GOLDEN GATE

THE COLE SUDDEN C.I.A. ACTION THRILLERS

SUDDEN KILL

THE HADRON ESCAPE

THAWED

CHILDREN'S BOOKS

THE PURLOINED PONIES

Made in the USA
Middletown, DE
04 June 2020